Dahling, If You Luv Me, Would You Please, Please Smile

Dahling, If You Luv Me, Would You Please, Please Smile

Rukhsana Khan

Stoddart Kids

TORONTO • NEW YORK

*We acknowledge the Canada Council for the Arts and the
Ontario Arts Council for their support of our publishing program.*

Published in Canada in 1999 by
Stoddart Kids,
a division of Stoddart Publishing Co. Limited
34 Lesmill Road
Toronto, Canada M3B 2T6
Tel (416) 445-3333 Fax (416) 445-5967
E-mail Customer.Service@ccmailgw.genpub.com

Published in the United States in 1999
by Stoddart Kids
a division of Stoddart Publishing Co. Limited
180 Varick Street, 9th Floor
New York, New York 14207
Toll free 1-800-805-1083
E-mail gdsinc@genpub.com

Distributed in Canada by
General Distribution Services
325 Humber College Blvd.
Etobicoke, Ontario Canada M3B 2T6
Tel (416) 213-1919 Fax (416) 213-1917
E-mail Customer.Service@ccmailgw.genpub.com

Distributed in the United States by
General Distribution Services
85 River Rock Drive, Suite 202
Buffalo, New York 14207
Toll free 1-800-805-1083
E-mail gdsinc@genpub.com

Canadian Cataloguing in Publication Data

Khan, Rukhsana
Dahling, if you luv me, would you please, please smile

ISBN 0-7737-6016-4

I. Title.

PS8571.H37D23 1999   jC813'.54   C98-931783-8
PZ7.K42Da   1999

Cover illustration by Chum McLeod
Text and cover design: Tannice Goddard

Printed and bound in Canada

Dedication

*To my excellent parents: Muhammad Anwar Khan and
Iftikhar Shahzadi Khan. Without their love and guidance
I would surely have strayed.*

Author's Note

All characters are fictional. Any resemblance to persons living or dead is purely coincidental.

1

I guess I'd always wanted to fit in. But mostly I couldn't afford it.

Deanford, being a public school, didn't have an official school uniform, but nine out of ten kids wore Lucky jeans. They were easy to spot, because of the little red tag sewn into the seam of the right rear pocket. Stupid place to put a tag. In order to read it you had to look at someone's bum.

Those jeans cost more than eighty dollars a pair. Just looking at them made me sick. At least 450 kids at Deanford wore Lucky's. What a waste. Especially when there were so many poor people going hungry.

Why would anyone pay that much for a pair of pants? I could just picture people twenty years from now looking back at us and thinking what fools we were, forking out that kind of money for something so dumb.

But if you wanted to be accepted, no other brand would do. And they had to have that little red tag, as small as your smallest fingernail, intact. There was a game the kids played where they tried to rip off each other's tags. If the label wasn't there, it meant you'd bought seconds, not first quality, and therefore you hadn't paid the full price.

I thought I was okay in my polyester pants. They looked like Lucky's, they had a zipper and pockets and beltloops, they just cost so much less. At least I dressed better than Premini Gupta, the only other "Indian" in the school.

Even if I'd wanted a pair of Lucky's, it would never have occurred to me to ask my parents for them. They had me, my older sister and the twins to provide for. Eighty dollars went a long way toward feeding us. I knew, I'd seen the grocery bills.

My polyester pants were scratchy, and when the static built up, they clung to my legs. But it wasn't until Art class one day that I realized they wouldn't do.

I was intent on my picture when I felt a hesitant tap on my elbow, and heard a whispered, "What's that you're drawing, Zainab?"

I looked up, straight into Jenny's baby blue eyes, or at least as much of them as I could see through her long stringy bangs. She sat beside me in most of my classes. She was one of the few girls that would. She was pretty except for her acne. Her complexion was a mass of angry red pimples in different stages of ripeness. Maybe that's why she let her ash blonde hair hang half over her face like a screen between her and the world. But what made the boys notice her were her breasts. They called her "Jenny-big-jugs" when she wasn't around.

She came to stand beside me. "That's an interesting picture, Zainab. What is it?"

I relaxed a little. She sounded sincere. "It's supposed to be hell."

Our art assignment had been to draw a picture using silhouettes. I'd made a stencil of a man's head in profile. It had a long sharp nose and a witch's pointed chin. It was supposed to be a devil. I'd traced and cut out two rows of them from black paper, highlighting the edges with grey as if it were charcoal turning to ash. I was just about to glue the cut-outs to a background of red, orange and yellow flames.

Jenny pushed aside some of her bangs and said softly, "It's kind of neat."

I flushed, mumbling a thanks.

"But maybe you could, I mean, why not make the chins and noses a little smaller? More human. It'll mean we all can end up in hell."

She had a point. I thanked her and trimmed the noses and chins to a decent length.

Kevin appeared. "Why do you have flames all the way to the top?"

"I think it says in the Quran that there'll be flames above and below. No escaping them."

He said, "Oh." He watched me add some white to

the black outlines for a moment then said, "You know, Zainab, I used to wear clothes like you."

I was too intent on my picture to notice the change in the tone of his voice. I muttered, "Really?"

"Yeah, then my dad got a job."

There was a burst of laughter from Kevin's friends. They just happened to be within earshot. I should have known.

At first I thought that Jenny was in on it. But through her curtain of hair I saw her face redden. In a gentle voice she said, "Oh, Kevin. That wasn't very nice."

Kevin's face grew still. The laughter died away. No one else could have said that to Kevin and gotten away with it. Now Kevin looked as uncomfortable as I felt. His mouth set in a grim line. He turned away. So did his followers.

What was wrong with my clothes? I wore a clean white blouse tucked into my grey polyester pants and a grey, black and white sweater over the blouse. I was co-ordinated, I was clean. I just didn't happen to be wearing Lucky's.

Jenny had a pair. They were so tight you could have read the year of a quarter in the back pocket. And she had on a tight sweater. Every line, every curve of her body was clear. From her slim hips and tiny waist to the dents in her shoulders where her straining bra straps cut into the flesh.

Premini Gupta sat across from me. When I looked up at her she quickly looked away, flicking aside her long black braid. She'd heard the whole thing but she too hadn't laughed, though for a different reason. She wore a faded calico dress, pink knee socks and a yellow cardigan that gave her brownish-yellow skin an even yellower tint. The sleeves of the cardigan were too short, revealing her bony wrists. If anyone dressed like her father was out of work, it was Premini. Why did they pick on me?

The very next day, Premini came to school in Lucky jeans. They were brand-new and so stiff she had trouble sitting down at her desk. There was a smirk on her face, and a wrinkle in her hooked nose as she looked me over. Now I was the only one in all grade eight who didn't own a pair of Lucky's.

I was standing in line to go in after recess when I overheard someone talking about the other reason the kids were ripping off tags. Apparently one of the stores was having a promotion — if you brought in twenty-two Lucky tags, you got a free pair of Lucky's.

I, too, began hunting tags.

At first, I stalked them openly, making a grab as Jenny walked past, her label hanging by a few threads, just begging to be torn off. But she turned on me. "You shouldn't rip tags. It's not fair. You don't have a tag anyone else can rip."

Her gentle reprimand was more embarrassing than if she'd yelled at me. And yet what she was saying wasn't fair. It seemed you couldn't rip tags unless you had one, and I couldn't get one unless I ripped tags. I'd have to be sneaky about it. Hunt them on the sly.

The only real opportunity was during Gym. In the middle of a soccer game, I told the teacher that I had to go to the bathroom. Then I snuck into the changeroom and coralled my prey. I wasn't stealing, I told myself. It was a game. I was just participating in a more efficient manner. It gave me particular satisfaction to rip off Cheryl's tag. She was Kevin's official girlfriend, though that didn't stop him from flirting with other girls. He called them his harem and he was constantly teasing them, pinching them, and touching them. Telling them that in the age of women's liberation it was their turn to carry his books to school. He said he liked to spread himself around.

Kevin would never treat me like that. He would never consider me pretty enough. In a way I was glad. If he had looked my way, if he had given me the attention he gave those girls, I don't know if I would have acted any differently than they did. There was no denying he was gorgeous. With platinum blonde hair and icy blue eyes.

Anyway, I was careful not to take all the tags. I was tempted to take Premini's but decided against it. It would be more logical to take the ones that were partially off, and Premini's hadn't had time to be torn at all. I'd get it later. I didn't take Jenny's either. Somehow it didn't feel right.

I gathered up nine tags, tucked them into my sock and ran back outside to join the game. But it was hard to keep a straight face when my classmates went into the changeroom and ranted about their lost tags. Jenny gave me a curious look. If she suspected anything she didn't say. I found the speckled pattern of the ceiling tiles extremely fascinating.

By mid-October, the cold weather made my

polyester pants cling to my legs in a static haze, squeaking where they rubbed together when I walked. It would be nice to have the feel of stiff denim next to my skin. We were doing track and field in Gym now and even when I was the first to finish my laps, I could only harvest two or three tags before the other kids started dragging themselves into the changeroom.

By the end of October, I had twenty-one tags. I only needed one more but it would be harder to come by. Kids were guarding their labels more carefully and I had a lot of competition. It seemed everyone was on the prowl for Lucky tags.

During Math one day, I saw an unguarded tag. The kids had left the closet wide open, with jackets and gym shorts spilling out onto the classroom floor. Mr. Weiss asked for a volunteer to clean up the mess. He picked me. While I was shoving the stuff back into the closet, I came across an old pair of cut-off jean shorts. They were Lucky's and they still had the tag intact!

I tucked them into the very bottom of the pile and nonchalantly closed the doors. I'd be back. I waited till recess and then, telling the teacher on yard duty that I had a stomach-ache, crept back up the stairs.

I had to walk past the classroom, as if on my way to the washroom, several times because whenever I was about to enter, a teacher or caretaker appeared. They always showed up when you didn't need them. Finally the hallway was empty.

Taking a deep breath, I slipped in. The shrieks and yells of the kids outside were muffled. I could barely hear them over the pounding of my heart.

The soles of my running shoes squeaked across the linoleum tiles as I made my way to the closet. My grey polyester pants crackled with static when I knelt down and dug through the discarded hats, scarves, mitts and T-shirts looking for the pair of cut-offs.

I found them. Turning them over, I smiled. Soon, very soon, I'd have the cool luxurious feel of stiff brand-new Lucky jeans against my legs. Very soon, even Kevin would no longer tease me about the way I dressed.

It was hot in the classroom. My hands were too sweaty to get a proper grip on the tag and I kept hearing footsteps creeping up behind me.

The tag kept slipping through my fingers, or else it was sewn on tighter than all the rest. I took off my jacket, my long hair clinging with static to the polyester lining like tentacles. Now my ponytail was glued across the back of my sweater. I tried to ignore it. The clock was ticking away. After a few more tugs at the stubborn tag, I dropped the shorts and freed my ponytail. Hair clung to my fingers and the sleeves of my sweater. I was hot from wrestling with my hair and the tag. What I needed was water. Yes. Water would be wonderful. It was so stuffy in the classroom.

I glimpsed the white face of the clock. 10:18. I snatched the shorts and bit the tag with my teeth, tearing it away from the pocket seam just as I heard footsteps outside the classroom doorway.

I searched the room for some escape. There was only the closet. I ducked inside, pulling some of the hats and scarves over me, just as the doorknob turned. I hadn't closed the closet door fully. It was Kevin and Jenny.

2

I felt visible, though the closet doors hid me well. I was sure Jenny could hear the pounding of my heart. She pushed aside her bangs and peered around the classroom. "Are you sure about this, Kevin? I don't think Mr. Weiss would like us to be in here during recess."

Kevin took a furtive peek down the hallway and quietly closed the door. "Relax, he'll never know."

Jenny dug her hands into her jacket pockets, hunching up her shoulders. "I don't like it. Maybe you could, I mean, just get your smokes and let's go."

Kevin stiffened. "Is this going to be a habit? You telling me what to do?"

Jenny's face was red. "But I, I didn't mean to."

"Like when I was kidding Zainab?"

"What?"

He twisted his face and mimicked her. "Oh, Kevin. That wasn't very nice."

Jenny said, "But, but, it wasn't."

Kevin rooted inside his desk till he found the pack of cigarettes. "Jeez, I was just joking. You showed me up in front of everyone."

Jenny put a hand on his arm. "I didn't mean to. It's just that . . ." Jenny looked down at the toe of her sneaker. "I'm sorry," she muttered.

"Don't let it happen again."

Jenny nodded quickly.

He reached an arm around her waist.

She slipped free and glanced at the clock. "Mr. Weiss will be here soon. We'd better go."

He pulled out a cigarette, put it in his mouth and lit it, all in one fluid gesture. Then, letting out a cloud of blue smoke, he gave Jenny a look that would melt any girl's heart. "What's your hurry?"

He must have rehearsed that look, those gestures, the whole scene. It was straight out of a corny western. But it was working. Jenny was practically drooling. Her baby blues were large and fixed on Kevin as he glided closer.

The closet was getting hotter. The smell of moldy sweaters and sweaty gym shorts was nauseating. Recess would be over soon and the chance of making a clean getaway was sinking with every tick of the clock.

He was feeling her up. His hands trying to release her sweater from her pants. Jenny backed away, whispering, "Please, Kevin. Please don't."

I could see her face, strained and agitated, as he concentrated further down her neckline. Why didn't she stop him?

What would it be like to have a boyfriend? My older sister, Layla, always laughed at the way girls fell for guys. We were lucky, she said. Islam spared us from that nonsense. Our parents would help choose our husbands. It was all practical, and it made sense. But . . . what would it be like to have the cutest guy in the school crazy about you?

He had her up against the chalkboard. The hand that held the cigarette was braced against it, trapping her. Gently, she was trying to push him away. "Please, Kevin. Please don't." Kevin didn't listen. Her voice took on a desperate note and a firmness I'd never heard before. "Kevin, no. No. STOP!"

He finally turned away with a sigh that spoke of frustration. Taking a long drag on his cigarette, he let it fall from his mouth, and crushed it with the toe of his sneaker. "I thought you liked me," he murmured, turning his back on Jenny. He was facing me, now. She couldn't see the way his eyes flicked back, measuring her.

Jenny stepped forward and touched the sleeve of his jacket. "Oh, Kevin, of course I like you."

Jenny didn't see the smirk, the barely contained laughter on Kevin's face, as she told him how much she cared. Kevin always said he would be a movie star one day. I had to admit he was a great actor already. He played her perfectly.

My hands were hurting. I looked down to see that

I'd been gripping the cut-off shorts so tightly my knuckles were white and cramped.

He was back at her, like a dog at a fire hydrant, and she, with a grimace of distaste, was tolerating it.

Why were girls such suckers for sweet talk? All any guy had to do was tell a girl what she wanted to hear and she'd do anything for him.

The click of the doorknob and the muffled voice of Mr. Weiss in the hallway made me sit up. Kevin, dragging Jenny by the hand, was rushing straight at me, heading for the only hiding place in the room. There was no time to dig deeper into the pile of stuff on the floor, no time to drag down the old discarded sweaters that still hung from the warped wire hangers above my head. He threw open the door and gaped at me, just as Mr. Weiss stepped into the room.

Kevin's eyes dropped to the shorts I was holding. I looked down to see a bit of tag peeking out through the fingers of my left hand. I moved my hand out of his line of vision, but not before he'd seen what I was holding, and figured out why I was in the closet. He turned with a boldness that was truly remarkable and said, "Look, Mr. Weiss, we caught Zainab stealing Lucky tags."

Mr. Weiss was frozen, one hand still resting on the doorknob, his saggy cheeks puffed out, his forehead puckered. Through the veil of Jenny's bangs, her eyes were wide and glued on me. Her pink lips framed a silent "Oh."

Kevin went on, sounding like a used car salesman,

"I just came in to get something, and Jenny came with me, then we heard this noise in the closet and there she was." He grabbed my hand, and despite me fighting him, managed to pry apart my fingers and dangle the tag in front of Mr. Weiss's face. "See. Caught her red-handed."

Mr. Weiss's gaze traveled from the crushed cigarette on the floor to Jenny's disheveled sweater and then back to Kevin. He took the tag from Kevin while opening the classroom door. "That's enough, Kevin. You and Jenny are excused."

Kevin smirked at me and headed for the door.

Mr. Weiss said, "Oh, and Kevin. This little incident doesn't leave this room. If I hear that anyone else knows about it, I'll just have to ask more about why you and Jenny were in here, unsupervised. Understand?"

Kevin nodded. The smirk faded a little but didn't disappear entirely.

Jenny gave me one quick apologetic glance and trailed Kevin out of the room.

Mr. Weiss closed the door firmly and sat down on the edge of a desk. "Unless you can explain to my satisfaction what you were doing in the closet, I'm afraid I'm going to have to contact your parents, Zainab."

There'd been a hum in my ears during this whole encounter, a kind of buzz, that was numbing. I was almost sure this was just a bad dream, convinced that nothing could really go this wrong, until he mentioned my parents. It was like a bucket of cold water thrown straight in my face. "Oh no, Mr. Weiss. You mustn't. I'm sorry. I'll never do it again, just please don't tell my parents."

He frowned at me. "Whatever were you stealing Lucky tags for?"

My face hot with shame, I muttered, "You wouldn't understand."

"Try me."

It was hard to begin, but once I did, the whole story came pouring out. I wondered, in the back of my mind, whether I should be spilling my guts like this, but I couldn't have stopped myself even if I'd tried. I told him about Kevin's remark, about Premini getting Lucky's, and about being the only kid in all grade eight without them.

He listened, his head bent, swinging the leg that dangled over the edge of the desk and nodding every now and then. When I'd finished, he asked, "But why did you steal the tags?"

I told him about the store promotion.

His face grew very still and he stared at me for a long moment. "But, Zainab, didn't you know that promotional offer is over? It was over a couple of months ago. Twenty-two Lucky tags won't get you anything now."

It was over? My chance was gone? I'd been sneaking around, stealing those stupid tags, all for nothing? The recess bell rang shrill and mocking as I stood there wishing the linoleum would open up and swallow me. I'd never felt so foolish in all my life, and what made things worse was that Mr. Weiss knew exactly how stupid I'd been.

He didn't ask why I hadn't just begged my parents for them. I guess he didn't need to. He was saying something.

"But why would you want to be like everyone else anyway? You're fine just the way you are."

"Are you kidding?" I asked. "I might as well be a leper, the way everyone avoids me."

He laughed, "You've been reading too many gothic romances, Zainab."

"Lepers aren't in gothic romances. And I don't read romances. Well, not only romances."

"Of course. Too many historical novels, then. You know what I mean. You're hardly a leper."

Tears welled up in my eyes. I cried, "You don't know what it's like not to have any friends in the whole school."

Mr. Weiss looked thoughtful. "What is it you really want, Zainab?"

I was taken aback. What did I want? Nobody had ever asked me before. It had never mattered. What did I want? I wiped my face on the back of my sleeve and said, "I want to be treated equally and fairly. I'm just as good as Kevin, or Cheryl or anyone else in this class and I want them to know it."

"Isn't it enough that you know it?"

"No."

Mr. Weiss opened his mouth to say something, looked puzzled, then closed it again. He picked up a pen, turned it over in his hands and then put it down. "Don't I treat you equally?"

"It's not you."

"Well, I know you're just as good as anyone in this class." He paused, a twinkle in his eye. "Or just as bad. But it's another thing proving it to others. You're better off just ignoring them. You were fine last year."

I muttered, "You sound like my parents. They told me to ignore them too. It doesn't work."

Mr. Weiss looked at the clock. "The other kids will be in soon. I don't have much time, but I've just had a thought. How do you like plays?"

"Well, I like Shakespeare, even though the language is difficult, and I tried Chekhov, but he's dull. All the characters ever do is sit around a table talking. My favorite is Tennessee Williams —"

"Let me rephrase that," said Mr. Weiss. "How good are you at writing plays?"

"You mean something like *The Glass Menagerie*? There's no way!"

"Oh, nothing that fancy!" Mr. Weiss's eyes came alive. He clapped his hands, lacing his fingers together. "How would you like to be in charge of the Mackenzie King play? It could be any story you want and you could choose whomever you want to play the lead. Though I do think you should stay away from classical literature," he said with a wry grin.

Deanford's students were divided by classes into four house leagues, four teams called Mackenzie King, Laurier, Pearson and MacDonald. Our class was in Mackenzie King.

"I don't know. Do you think I can do it?"

He fixed me with a measuring look, then nodded. "Yes, I do. I wouldn't be giving you this responsibility if I didn't. But the main thing is, you'd be in charge. The other kids will have to come to you. It's a chance to make friends and to prove yourself."

"Or make a fool of myself."

He said, "I'll be here if you need any help."

"But what if we lose? All the kids will blame me."

He shrugged. "That's a chance you'll have to take. It's either this or ignore them for the rest of the year. This is your last year here anyway, then you're off to high school. You might not see any of them again. They might go to a different school, but then again they might not. It's up to you. You can ignore the problem or meet it head on."

The classroom door opened and the kids came marching in. Mr. Weiss got up from the desk saying, "Let me know tomorrow."

I stopped him. I felt like I'd plunged off the edge of a great cliff. "I don't need to think about it. I'll do it."

He grinned at me, patting me on the shoulder. "That's the spirit."

3

All the way home, I thought about the play and the more I thought about it, the more I liked the idea. I'd never been in charge of a play before. In fact, whenever we performed the Christmas pageant, I was never anything more than a tree, dressed in a brown suit, holding a bunch of green branches. And when I asked why I couldn't be Mary or a shepherd, the teacher told me not to be silly, I was the perfect shade for tree bark.

Kevin and all the other popular kids would have to deal with me in order to be in the play. If we worked together, maybe they'd see that I wasn't so bad.

I turned onto our street with mixed feelings. I gazed at the cloudy sky and made a dua, a little prayer, asking God to make Layla late. Have her miss her bus, anything, so I didn't have to face her right away. It was a hopeless exercise. Layla was never late for anything in her life. She even woke up five minutes before the alarm every morning. Don't know why she even bothered setting it.

I slipped into the front hallway. The door creaked loudly. Startling me. I tiptoed down the stairs and sat on the sofa in the T.V. room. So far so good. Five minutes later, my muscles were just starting to recover from the long walk home when Layla barged in, her hands on her hips, her black eyes flashing. "Did you pray yet?"

She was referring to Zuhr prayer. As Muslims, we have to pray five times a day, and Zuhr is the one after lunch. We're the only Muslims in school. Our father doesn't want to make any waves. He says we can pray it when we get home, even though it's late.

Layla looked at me beneath those long, thick eyelashes of hers. Only two of us kids were born with those eyelashes. Her and Waleed, my brother. It's a pity. Eyelashes like that are wasted on a boy!

"What are you sitting in the dark for? Hiding?"

I didn't say anything.

"Well? Aren't you supposed to say something when you get home?"

I remained silent.

She said, "The Prophet, peace be upon him, said the one who enters must greet the ones who are already there."

I interrupted. "He also said the one who is standing should greet the one sitting, so you were supposed to say it when you came into the room."

"But you were supposed to say it when you got home, so it's your responsibility first."

I didn't feel like arguing any more. "Assalaamu alaikum," I muttered obediently.

"I didn't hear you."

"Assalaamu alaikum," I said more loudly.

"Wa alaikum assalam," she replied with a smile. She'd tricked me. By replying to my greeting she didn't have to greet me in the room. I know it's silly but it bugged me. Made me burn inside.

"Did you pray yet?" she asked again.

"I just got home."

She shrugged. "Don't you think it will please God if you pray to Him before tending to your own selfish needs?"

"Can't I rest a few more minutes? It was a long walk."

Layla turned and shrugged. Over her shoulder she remarked, "It's up to you, I guess. But it does show where your priorities lie."

Darn! I couldn't relax anymore. It took exactly four minutes to pray the four rakats of Zuhr. I guess it won't hurt to pray first and then rest, I thought. I raced through the prayer, the Arabic words a blur on my tongue. I was on my third rakat when I heard a footstep behind me. I knew it was Layla come to check if I was praying correctly. I stiffened and slowed my lips enough so that she could pick out the words of the prayer. Her ear was almost brushing my cheek, checking to see that I wasn't just pretending. If I hadn't been praying, I'd have pushed her away. She nodded as if satisfied and took a step back. I breathed a little easier. It was time to bow down, my face to the floor, my nose and forehead touching it. I could feel her come down beside me. Layla said, "Your nose isn't touching."

I couldn't tell her that it was, not while I was praying. Besides, it was useless arguing with her. If Layla believed your nose wasn't touching, then it wasn't. I was bowing down for the second time, when I felt a foot on my butt.

"Get your bum down!" she commanded.

I hunkered down, cramped and uncomfortable.

For a while she said nothing, and when I finished the fourth set of prostrations and was sitting and finishing the prayer, she finally left.

When I was done, I tore off my scarf, and crashed onto the couch. I don't hate Layla, really I don't. It's just that I don't really like her. I don't like her a lot. A Muslim isn't supposed to hate her sister. Layla would say it was un-Islamic and she'd be right. She's always right about such things. Oh, why bother with all that? I should be thinking about the play. What story to do. How to win that competition.

I pictured myself the director, holding auditions like I'd seen in the movies. Sitting three rows back in a huge theatre, in the comfortable darkness, while Kevin squirmed on stage, trying to remember his lines. Sweat dripping from his chalk-white brow as he squinted past the stage lights, trying to gauge my reaction. I laughed a deep rich laugh, a benevolent, magnanimous laugh. I was in the mood to be generous. Relax,

I told him. Just take it from the top of scene one, one more time.

But what play would we perform? I chewed my lip. My eyes rested on the Quran. It's to Muslims what the Holy Bible is to Christians and the Torah is to Jews. I didn't really expect to get an idea for a play but when I opened it, I came to the story of Joseph. Every night my father read a section of the Quran to us and every night we hated it, except when he came to the story of Joseph. The Arabic was almost poetry and even the English translation was rhythmic and melodious. The "thee's" and "thou's" of the Old English took me to another world. I was enjoying the chapter, living the ancient story.

I barely heard Ami, my mother, come downstairs with the twins. Layla barged into the room again.

"What are you reading now?"

"For your information, I'm reading Quran, now leave me alone."

"But there's work to be done."

From the kitchen my mother called, telling Layla not to disturb me if I was reading Quran, and to do the work herself.

I resisted the urge to stick out my tongue, but Layla's red face gave me a lot of satisfaction before she left the room. I finished the story of Joseph by the time my father got home. The ideas, images and language soaked into me so that I felt if I just closed my eyes I'd be back in time, in the rich, hot land of Egypt.

By the time I sat down for supper, I'd decided what play we'd perform. Joseph, so handsome and good, able to interpret dreams, was everything I'd ever wanted to be. Wronged by his jealous brothers and sold into slavery, but victorious in the end. What an adventurous life he'd led.

My father murmured the brief prayer before eating — it means "In the name of God with the blessings of God" — and was just about to begin his meal, when I cleared my throat and said in my most solemn, dignified voice, "O my father. Could we not have a more detailed grace before we eat of the food our Lord has provided?"

My father exchanged glances with my mother. Layla rolled her eyes and said, "Oh, brother."

I turned to her. "Verily, I but wish to share a prayer of peace and prosperity with the rest of my family."

My father watched me, his bearded chin cupped in the palm of his bony hand, his black eyes twinkling. "Go ahead."

The twins, little Waleed and Seema, nibbled at their chapatis. I frowned at them, but forgave them, they were only five years old. I began, "O gracious Lord of the Worlds. Grant us, thy servants, of Thy infinite bounty and wisdom in all our endeavors . . ." I went on for a while, ignoring my father's rumbling stomach. Layla's foot tapped a beat on the floor. I would have given her a dirty look, but I couldn't catch her eye.

We were having stewed chicken for supper. It swam in a hearty sauce of coriander and turmeric. The aroma of the fresh coriander leaves drifted up, enveloping us, tantalizing our nostrils, making even my mouth water. I tried to focus on the words I said, liking the way the language rolled off my tongue. I felt like the narrator in the movie *The Ten Commandments.*

Layla nudged me in the ribs after a while. I ignored her. Then she kicked me in the shin. I yelped and ended the prayer. Immediately, everyone attacked their food. I broke my chapati with dignity and dipped it slowly into the curried dish in front of me. This was how Joseph would have eaten. And though I lived several millenia after him, the food I ate was also similar to his.

After supper, while she washed the dishes and I rinsed, Layla gave me a curious look. "What's with you tonight? You look like the cat that swallowed the canary. Did something happen at school?"

I felt like I was going to burst. I had to tell someone so I told her about the play.

She stared at me, her mouth hanging open. "He asked you to produce a play?"

"Yeah."

"He must have been desperate."

I didn't say anything, but she read my face and said in exasperation, "I'm only joking! Can't you take a joke? Sheesh!" She scraped some bones into the garbage can and soaped the dish. "What play are you thinking of doing?"

I took the dish she handed me, muttering, "Never mind."

She stopped scrubbing and looked at me. "You can tell me."

"You'll just laugh."

"I'll try not to."

"You always laugh."

She shrugged and continued scrubbing. "Suit yourself."

We worked in a heavy silence for a while. I kept glancing at her for signs of impatience. There were none. Calmly, she continued washing the dishes, scraping with her nail at a bit of crusted food, not caring in the least whether I told her or not.

"Okay," I said, "I'll tell you but you have to promise not to tell anyone else. I want it to be a surprise for Ami and Abi."

"Sure."

"We're going to do the story of Joseph."

She stopped washing, her hands submerged in the soapy water, and stared at me. "You mean the story of the prophet Joseph, peace be upon him?"

I nodded.

"You can't do a prophet's story as a play. You can't portray a prophet."

"Why not?"

"It just isn't done."

"Why not?"

"Don't be so stupid. That's as bad as Charlton Heston playing Moses, peace be upon him, in *The Ten Commandments*. In one movie he's Moses, peace be upon him, in the next he's a bank robber with a love scene. It's disrespectful to Moses, peace be upon him. How can anyone pretend to be a prophet? They were special. Examples for us to follow. Ask Abi if you don't believe me. He'll tell you."

"Fine, I will." I shut off the tap right there and then

and went into the living room to ask my father. He said Layla was right.

When I came back into the kitchen, Layla grinned. "I told you so."

I felt like throwing the dish towel at her. Instead I returned to the sink and finished rinsing the dishes.

After a while Layla said, "You could do a play about a hadith if you wanted. You know, a saying of the Prophet, peace be upon him."

Through clenched jaws I said, "I know what a hadith is."

She tossed her head. The tip of her long black ponytail flicked me in the face, but she didn't notice. "There's lots of good stories in there. And as long as you don't portray the Prophet, peace be upon him, or one of his companions you should be fine."

I didn't feel like doing the play at all anymore.

4

Halfway to school the next day, I heard someone call me. I turned to see Jenny running to catch up. She really shouldn't run. She clutched her binder tight, but even under the jacket, her chest was bouncing as if jogging with a life of its own. She arrived breathless.

"I'm so glad I caught you. I hate walking to school alone."

I walked a little slower so she'd have a chance to catch her breath. It was very windy. My hair whipped my face. I kept having to push it behind my ears. I said, "I didn't know you lived around here. Which is your house?"

"It's back there. It really isn't anything special."

She had waved in the direction of a shabby old

street, a dead end, with a railway line running behind the houses. The dandelions on the overgrown lawns were grey-haired and balding. The wind made them nod, scattering their seeds in all directions.

For several blocks we walked without talking. Leaves and crumpled bits of paper blew past us. I didn't step on any cracks in the sidewalk. It was a stupid little game I played. Jenny stepped on ten.

She broke the silence. "I guess you must have seen what happened in the classroom yesterday. You know, I mean, between Kevin and me."

I nodded without looking at her. From the corner of my eye I could see that her face was a deep red.

"Um. I'd really appreciate it, I mean, I'd really like it if you wouldn't mention it to anyone. I mean, that you saw us together. You know, Cheryl might get mad."

I stared at her then. I'd been so embarrassed about being caught with the tags I'd almost forgotten about her and Kevin.

Her hair, wispy and light, blew in her face and hid her eyes. "You see, Kevin doesn't want anyone to know. About us, I mean. Not yet. Not till he dumps Cheryl."

"Don't worry, Jenny. Besides, who'd I tell?"

"I'm so glad, Zainab. I'd just die it if it were all over the school. I just couldn't stand it."

"Don't worry. I won't tell. I promise."

"Oh, thanks. Thanks so much. And don't worry about the tags. I won't tell anyone about them. And I made Kevin promise he wouldn't tell either."

I didn't believe Kevin would keep it a secret and I guess my disbelief showed.

Jenny said, "No, really. You don't have to worry."

We rounded the corner, and Deanford was in sight. Jenny said, "I hope you didn't get in too much trouble after Weiss let us go."

"No. I was lucky."

"How?"

I looked at her. Her bangs still veiled her face. She reminded me of a shaggy sheepdog. How could I not trust her? I said, "Mr. Weiss was going to call my parents but I managed to talk him out of it."

"You're kidding! How?"

I shrugged. "It wasn't too hard. In fact, he gave me a kind of assignment. I'm in charge of the Mackenzie King play for the drama competition."

"You're kidding! Can I help?"

Alarm bells rang too late in my mind. What did she mean by help? She couldn't act worth beans. "Uh. I don't know. What did you want to do?"

As if she could read my mind, she said, "Oh, I don't want a part in the play. I'd just like to, you know, be your assistant, that kind of thing."

"I don't think so. I've decided not to take the job."

"Why not? You'd probably be good at it."

Layla's laughing face flashed across my mind's eye. I'd thought I'd be good at it too, before I'd talked to her.

Lightly, Jenny touched my arm. "You should do it. Show them all what you've got."

I almost smiled. Part of me agreed. I shook my head. It was too risky. As we stepped onto school property, the bell rang and we were ushered inside.

In the classroom, I went up to Mr. Weiss, tapping him on the elbow.

He was chatting with another teacher and gave me a 'not right now' look. I went and sat down.

As soon as he was finished with the teacher, I started forward, but he gestured for us all to quiet down and remain seated.

He faced us, pulling up his pants and tucking in the tails of his shirt. "I've got news. I've finally decided who will be in charge of the play this year."

I stuck up my hand, waving it frantically. Mr. Weiss smiled at me. "It's okay, Zainab." He turned back to the class. "As you know, Mackenzie King has never won the house league competitions since the formation of this school twenty-eight years ago." He chuckled. "Some even say we're cursed." He pulled up his pants again and tucked in his shirt tails. "This year it looks as though we have a chance. Especially since I've put Zainab here in charge of the play."

The kids groaned. They actually groaned. As if they were one human body being told they had four months to live. I wanted to sink down into my seat, become one with the grain of the wood. Mr. Weiss was furious at them.

"That's enough! I'll have no more of that. Zainab is in charge and I expect all of you to give her your full co-operation!"

Kevin stood up, his icy blue eyes flashing a look of contempt at me. "Why? Why put her in charge when we finally have a chance? Especially in drama. We've got the best actors of the school in our class."

He was referring to himself. He'd appeared in a few commercials and had a couple of small roles in movies. Once he played a paperboy, telling some detective where the crooks had gone. In the whole movie all he said was, "That way, sir." And pointed. The other time he shined shoes and was tossed a quarter by the star. He had to tip his hat, but not say anything. If anyone else had done it, they would have been teased to death, but not Kevin. No one ever made fun of Kevin. It was kind of funny though, if you thought about it. He'd never had a paper route or shined shoes in his life.

Everybody was agreeing with him. One of Kevin's gang stood up too and said, "Yeah, with Kevin we're sure to win."

Mr. Weiss frowned at him and turned to Kevin. "In that case, Zainab's job should be easy. Think of it as a challenge to your artistic abilities. You of all people should appreciate that, Kevin. And if you're serious about acting, then you'll have to learn to get along with all kinds of directors. What better time to learn than right now?"

Kevin grumbled but sat down.

Mr. Weiss gave a satisfied nod. "Well then. Since that's settled, take out your history books to page fifty-seven and read till the end of the chapter."

There were rumblings, like mutiny in the ranks, as everyone shuffled through their textbooks, then a loud slam.

Mr. Weiss jumped. "Kevin!"

Kevin was picking his textbook up off the floor.

"Sorry, sir, my text accidentally fell."

It was clear Mr. Weiss thought it was no accident. "Don't let it happen again."

Mr. Weiss came over to my desk. "You wanted to say something, Zainab?"

"Oh, nothing." I picked up my text and started reading. During the whole lesson I could hardly concentrate. Finally, the recess bell rang and everyone started filing out the door. Mr. Weiss called me to stay behind.

After the last kid was gone, he said, "What did you want to say to me?" His eyes were a soft brown. "Go on, you can say anything."

Up close, you could see the puffy bags under his eyes, and the wrinkles at the corners of his mouth. He looked tired. As if he had a pile of his own problems. I couldn't back out now. I just couldn't, not when he had such faith in me.

"I just don't know what play we should do."

His eyes lit up. "Well, you know, I was thinking. This is a wonderful opportunity to expand our horizons. Why don't you take a story from your culture and make a play from that?"

"Wouldn't that just give them more stuff to make fun of me with?"

He shrugged. "It's really up to you. You can do a regular story if you wish. It was just a suggestion. Is that any help?"

It wasn't, but I smiled and when he asked me if I had any more questions I shook my head and left.

Jenny was waiting for me outside. "So, are you

going to do it? Are you? And can I be your assistant? Please?"

"Yeah, I guess so."

She was skipping along beside me. I felt like slapping her. She said, "So what play are you going to do?"

"I don't know. That's what I was talking to Weiss about. He thinks I should do something about my culture."

Jenny grabbed my arm. "That's a great idea. It would be so fresh and different. You must have tons of stories to tell."

Who'd ever want to hear what a Paki had to say, and a girl Paki at that?

We rounded the corner of the school, straight into the stiff wind. It pelted us with grains of sand and blew in our ears. We found a sheltered cranny where it couldn't reach us so well. I saw a kid strut by, wearing Lucky jeans with the tag intact. I had the beginnings of an idea. I said, "Maybe we could do a play about how useless fashion is. I mean it really is stupid. One year short skirts are in, the next year they're not. I mean, who decides when they look good and when they don't? People should wear what they want to."

Jenny nodded thoughtfully. "What about that story about the king who was tricked by those tailors into paying for imaginary clothes?"

I nodded. "I know the one. I can't remember the title, though."

She said, "You know, the tailors kept saying how beautiful the material was and everyone, even the king, was too embarrassed to say he couldn't see it."

I nodded again. "And when the king went parading through the streets in his new clothes, no one told him all they could see was his underwear. Until a kid said, 'Look, the —' Now I remember! It wasn't a king at all, it was an emperor. It was called *The Emperor's New Clothes*."

Jenny laughed. "That's it. It would be great."

"Nah. I'd never get anyone to parade around in the nude."

Jenny looked serious. "Well, I don't know. Maybe not nude, but in their underwear. Besides, well, what I mean is, not everyone is against being naked." She glanced at me and frowned. "Don't look at me like that. I'm not talking about me. I'm just saying some people like the feeling of wearing no clothes. You know, they don't think it's any big deal. And in the art galleries, there's lots of pictures . . . What I mean is that the human body is beautiful. Some people don't mind showing it off."

"What are you talking about, Jenny? Do you . . ."

Jenny blushed a deep red. "Of course not! Don't be silly. But my mom belongs to a club and they . . ."

The only image of a mother I could think of was my own. And the idea of a bunch of chubby, saggy naked women on lounge chairs almost made me gag.

"Why would she do that?"

Jenny looked grim. "Even if you don't agree with it, you don't have to act like that!"

I caught myself. "I'm sorry. I didn't mean it."

Jenny had her arms crossed beneath her huge

breasts as she stared out over the field in the direction of Kevin. I was respectfully silent, and soon the lines of her shoulders eased and her eyes softened.

I wouldn't have dared bring up the subject again, though I was dying to know more.

Surprisingly, Jenny went on. "My mother thinks that she'll find a nice man at this club."

I didn't say anything. Not one word. My gut told me it was the right thing to do.

5

I thought about the play all during the long, cold, wet walk home. Jenny was with Kevin. The sky was the color of steel wool, and the wind, which had been almost playful this morning, was driving needles of rain against every soaked inch of me.

It was a relief to get home and peel wet polyester off my clammy legs. I put on some warm clothes and went to pray. I would need all the help I could get.

I collapsed on the sofa and a few moments later, Layla barged in, as usual. "Have you prayed yet? Prayer time is going."

"Yes."

She stopped and looked at me. "What?"

"Yes, I prayed, now leave me alone."

She narrowed her eyes. "You're being disrespectful. I am your elder and you're supposed to respect anyone older than you."

"You're only a year older."

"For your information, I'm nineteen months older. Besides, it makes no difference. Prophet Muhammad, peace be upon him, said you have to respect your elders. He didn't say you only had to respect them if they were a lot older."

All this twisted logic made my brain hurt. I didn't have the energy to argue. I rubbed my head and said more respectfully, "Would you please not bother me then? I had a rough day."

Instead of leaving she came and sat in front of me. "Was it the play? You're not doing the story of Prophet Joseph, are you?"

"Yes and no."

"What is it? Yes or no?"

I sighed and put my arm down to look at her. "Yes, it was the play and no, I'm not doing the story of Joseph."

"That's Prophet Joseph, peace be upon him."

"Prophet Joseph."

"Peace be upon him."

I took a deep breath and said, "Prophet Joseph, peace be upon him."

She tilted her head, letting her thick black hair fall to one side, and looked at me speculatively. "Then which story are you doing?"

My head was throbbing and she'd cornered me. I didn't want to tell her. She'd just laugh at me. I was so tired! Darn! Why did she always have to boss me around?

In a calm, even voice, with no hint of attitude, I said, "With all due respect, I'd rather not say."

Her mouth hung open for just a moment, then she narrowed her eyes and shrugged. "Fine. Don't tell me. I was just trying to help but it's obvious you don't want any help. I just thought that since I starred in my grade eight play, and our house league won, you might want some help. But no, you think you know it all. So fine. I just didn't want you to make a fool of yourself. But if that's what you want to do, you go right ahead."

I'd forgotten about that. She'd played Marilla Cuthbert in their play, *Anne of Green Gables*. It wasn't quite the starring role, she'd tried out for Anne, but the kids in charge just couldn't imagine a brown-skinned Anne. Maybe she could help. "Okay," I said, "I'll tell you."

She gawked at me, her brows arched high. "What makes you think I still want to know?"

"We're doing the story of *The Emperor's New Clothes*."

"That fairy tale? I thought you were doing a hadith."

"No."

"I was sure you were doing a hadith."

"No, I never said that."

She shook her head, her forehead puckered. "I could have sworn you were doing a hadith."

I gritted my teeth to stop myself saying something I was going to regret.

She tapped her finger on the tip of her chin, gazing at the ceiling tiles. "Well, if you ask me, I think you should do a hadith."

I got up and went to see if my mother needed any help with supper.

We were having karayla. Sometimes it's called bitter melon curry, and some people call it bitter gourd. A lot of work. I was kept busy rubbing salt on the karayla and squeezing to get out the bitterness, and then my mom gave me a bunch of onions to cut. It was still better than talking to Layla.

So I sat there, my eyes burning, cutting onions — not too thick, my mother kept reminding me — and my foot fell asleep. It would be at that moment that my father came home.

"Assalaamu alaikum," he called, tramping down the stairs. He saw me wincing as I stretched and asked, "What's wrong?"

My foot was all pins and needles. I whispered, "My foot's asleep."

My father wore a sympathetic frown. He looked so concerned. "Which foot is it?"

I moved my right foot. With a mischievous grin on his face, he tried to tap it with his toe. Quickly I got up and hobbled around, trying to stay out of reach while he chased me. He was too quick. He caught me and poked my foot with his big toe. I doubled over in tingling agony, laughing hard.

"There," he said. "That should wake it up."

When we sat down for dinner, my father held up his hands in dua. "In the name of God with the blessings of God." He was about to dig in, when he looked at me, one bushy eyebrow raised. "Did you want to say a longer dua?"

I shook my head. "No, that's okay."

He grinned at my mother and everyone began eating. For a while there was silence.

Layla looked back and forth from my mother to my father. Finally she said, "If a Muslim kid is doing a play at school, and she could do any play she wanted, shouldn't she do a play about a hadith or something else about Islam?"

I glared at her, warning her to stop. She ignored me.

My father wiped some curry from his bearded chin. "Why?"

Layla shrugged, tearing a piece of roti to ribbons. "It's her responsibility. What better opportunity to teach them about Islam?"

My ears burned and I hunched down in my seat. It seemed Layla was determined to turn me into a preacher.

My father frowned. "I suppose so."

Layla smirked at me. "See?"

I faced her. I could feel the twin's eyes darting back and forth between me and Layla, like it was a tennis match. I said, "You didn't do a hadith in your house league play."

Layla looked uncomfortable. "It wasn't . . . ahem, up to me."

"That's because the teacher didn't pick you to be the director!"

Layla's face turned red. She said nothing but piled her strips of roti till they formed a wall.

My father's eyebrows were drawn together in disapproval. I knew I should stop, but I couldn't. "Just because I get the chance to be director, doesn't mean you should spoil it with your lousy suggestions. If I need help, I'll ask!"

Layla covered her face, burst into sobs, and ran from the table. The twins mouths were o's of surprise. My mother looked worried. My father looked ominous.

His voice whipped me with gale force fury. "For shame, Zainab! She's only trying to help. How could you be so cruel?"

"But, Abi, she's been bothering me since yesterday. I tried to tell her nicely but she wouldn't listen."

"Enough! That you should treat your older sister with such disrespect. And that you should do so right in front of me! Have you no shame?!"

I stared down at my hands in my lap. I dared not ask if it would have been better if I'd done it behind his back.

"After your mother and me, she is in charge over you. You don't know how lucky you are. She has responsibilities. And she cares very much for you and only wants you to do well with that silly play of yours. Why should she suggest things, unless she wants good for you? And look at the way you treated her."

Quietly I said, "I'm sorry, Abi."

"Hmph. It's not to me you should be saying sorry. It's to her, getting down on your knees and begging forgiveness."

From the corner of my eye I saw my mother shaking her head quickly.

My father relented. "Fine, you don't need to get on your knees. Just say you're sorry and don't ever speak to her in such a tone again!"

I nodded. "Gee, Abi." I pushed away from the table. The chair legs scraped against the linoleum with a shuddering groan, a sound of disapproval.

I found Layla sprawled facedown on her bed, in the room we shared. She'd stopped crying. The room was silent. And she was so still I stared hard to see if she was breathing.

"Layla?"

Slowly she rolled over. Her face settled into a hurt look, her long thick eyelashes drooping, her lower lip trembling. "Come to rub it in some more, Miss Director of the House League Play?"

"Sorry about that."

"You don't sound too sorry to me."

"I am sorry. I shouldn't have said that."

"You're not really sorry. You're only saying it because Abi made you."

She was right, but I couldn't say so. "No, really," I lied. "I am truly sorry for saying that stuff about the director. It was cruel."

She sat up, curling her arms around her knees, tossing back her long black hair. "You don't have to play games with me, Zainab. I know when you're lying. But it's okay. You don't have to be sorry. I won't tell on you. In fact, if Abi asks me if you apologized, I'll say yes. Even though we both know you didn't really mean it."

"I said I'm sorry. What more do you want?"

"Oh, Zainab. I should have stopped. I should have just let it go. You're angry now."

I gritted my teeth, then made myself stop. It wouldn't be very convincing to say I was sorry through clenched teeth. I tried to put a sincere look on my face. It was so sincere it hurt. "I'm not angry, Layla. I wish you'd believe me. I really and truly am sorry."

She looked at me for a moment. Measuring me. I continued looking sincere, though I was sure any minute my face would crack with the effort. Finally she relaxed. "All is forgiven."

I heaved a sigh of relief, and turned to go back to my supper. My roti was cold and the karayla was bitter.

6

Layla and I shared a room, but most nights she didn't come to bed right away. She'd have these long conversations with my parents, then barge in, turning on the light, disturbing my sleep. I'd started waiting up for her so she wouldn't wake me. I was waiting for her tonight. She was taking longer than usual. And I got to thinking how lucky she was. Being the oldest, she was forever bossing me and the twins around.

And she'd had my parents all to herself for a whole year — nineteen months — before I was born. She never got hand-me-downs. My father lavished the most attention on her.

What was good about being second? Nothing.

Ten minutes went by and she still hadn't come. I

yawned so wide my ears popped. Gosh I was tired. Another full day tomorrow. How was I going to start the auditions?

But I couldn't think of all that. Where was Layla? She should have been here by now. I slipped out of bed and up the stairs. All was dark. I passed the twins' rooms, grumbling to myself. Why did they each get their own room and we didn't? Of course, Waleed, being the only boy, needed his privacy. And Seema would raise a fuss. So Layla and I had to double-up.

There were quiet voices coming from my parents' room. Silently I crept within earshot. I felt wicked. I'd never done anything like this before. I was sure I'd be caught, like yesterday in the closet with the jeans' tag in my hands. I never had any luck being bad. Kneeling on the floor, so my parents wouldn't notice me, I peeked into their room.

Layla was standing with her back to the door, a black silhouette against the light from the tiny bedside lamp. My father was sitting up in bed, my mother was lying down, watching.

My father said, "Did you redo that math test?"

Layla shifted position from one foot to the other. Finally she said, "No, Abi gee."

"Why not?"

"I only got three wrong, and I know what I did wrong, so I don't see why I should have to write those questions out. The teacher never asked me to. And none of the other kids' parents tell them to."

"I am not one of the other kids' parents."

"I know, Abi gee. But as long as I know what I did

wrong, I won't make the mistakes again, I promise."

"It was careless to make the mistakes in the first place. We cannot afford to make even one mistake. The whites can, but not us," said my father, exasperation in his voice. My mother reached out her hand and touched his arm. My father sighed. "Have it for me tomorrow."

"Gee, Abi," she said, hanging her head. Was she going to head back to our room? I sat up, ready to crawl down the hall. But there was no need. Layla didn't leave.

My father said, "Do not look like that, Layla. Do not be sad."

Layla sniffed. "You never make Zainab redo all her tests and assignments. You never care if she makes mistakes. She shows you her report card and whatever it is, you say, 'That's good. Atchi bethi.' With me you always ask, 'Was it the highest in the class?' And even if it is the highest, if it's ninety-eight percent, you say, 'What happened to the other two percent?' It's not fair."

My father smiled. "If I am hard on you, it's because I expect more from you. It's not easy to be the oldest. I know. But they say in Pakistan, if the first row of bricks is straight, then the wall will be straight."

"What does that mean?" asked Layla.

My father laughed. "It means that when you're building a wall, you have to make sure the bottom row is straight, so you work really hard on that row to make it perfect. Then the other rows are easy. You are an example to your sisters and brother. So I want you to be the best you can be."

At this Layla perked up a bit.

My father continued, "If I criticize you, it's because I love you. I do not like to see you make the mistakes that I made. Remember the saying, 'Only your best friends will tell you how rotten you really are.' It's true. Only they would take the care to help you improve."

Layla drooped a little. "Gee, Abi," she muttered.

My mother sat up. "Don't worry, bethi, you're getting better every day."

That sounded like a dismissal to me. As quietly as I could, I scampered down the hall on all fours and then, at a safe distance, I ran. I made it back to my bed a moment before Layla barged in.

She spent ten minutes washing her face, putting on zinc oxide for her imaginary pimples and then coating it with a layer of baby powder. She did this every night, coming to bed looking like a Japanese geisha. I'd learned not to say anything.

She sat down on her bed. My hand hovered over the lamp, aching to shut it off and go to sleep, but I also wanted to say something.

I cleared my throat. Layla looked up from rubbing Vaseline on her feet.

"You know, Layla, I guess I don't say this much. But I'm glad you're my older sister."

Layla's jaw hung open for a fraction of a second, then her eyes narrowed with distrust. "What do you mean?"

"Oh, nothing. It's just that it must be hard to be the oldest. You know. Abi and Ami count on you more than the rest of us. And Abi's kind of hard on you."

"He is not!"

"I only meant —"

"I know what you meant. But you're wrong. They depend on me because I'm dependable. Not like you. Hmph."

She grabbed a large gob of Vaseline and massaged the sole of her foot vigorously. "You make yourself scarce when there's work to be done."

I ignored that. "I just want to say that I know you work hard. I just want to say I appreciate it. I just wish — No, from now on, I will work harder to help."

"Well, well. Maybe there's hope for you after all."

"What do you mean?"

Layla closed the Vaseline lid with a snap. "I really shouldn't be telling you, it's kind of a secret between Abi and me."

"What?"

She got up and put the Vaseline back on the dresser. I could see her reflection watching me in the mirror.

"What?" I said.

"Well, if you must know, Abi's been helping me improve myself. Every night he tells me the things I need to improve on."

"Oh," I said, pulling the covers up to my chin. I was ready to sleep now. I didn't want to hear anymore of this. But Layla didn't take the hint.

"I've been thinking. I could do that for you. You know how Abi says that only your best friends will tell you how rotten you really are?"

I didn't like the sound of this. I hated that saying.

Layla took off her slippers and slid under her

covers. "Well, I think it's about time you tried to improve yourself."

Layla switched off the light herself, so she didn't see the look of horror on my face.

She continued, "Every night, I'll tell you all your faults. That way you can work on improving them."

If I argued with her, we'd be up all night.

"Well?" she said.

"Why can't Abi tell me if I have any faults?"

"If?" Layla laughed. "Oooh. Aren't we Miss Perfect!"

"I, I mean. You know what I mean."

"Well, for one thing, Abi's too busy. And for another, he says that if you make the first row of bricks straight, then the whole wall will be straight. I'm the first row of bricks, you see. So since he's working on me, he doesn't need to be bothered with you."

The darkness was complete. I was glad she couldn't see my face. It almost seemed, from the way she'd said it, that Abi didn't want to be bothered with me.

"He works hard enough already. You don't want to give him extra work, do you?"

"No. Of course not."

"Besides, I know your faults a lot better than he does. I'm the one who's got to put up with them."

Did I have that many that she had to 'put up' with them? I managed to keep my voice steady when I said, "Okay."

Layla took a deep breath. "For one thing, you're very selfish."

I almost sat up in bed. Selfish? If she'd said I was lazy and always trying to get out of housework, she would've had a point. But selfish? I said, "What do you mean? When was I selfish?"

"Remember when I had to take you to that birthday party?"

I stifled a giggle. I remembered all right. It was the first birthday party Layla had ever been invited to. I kicked up such a fuss that my mother made her take me along. We each got a goody bag to take home. I ate all my candy right away but Layla saved her big red lollipop. The next morning, I got up early to watch cartoons and saw her lollipop in the fridge. I did try not to eat it but there it was, propped up, looking at me every time I opened the fridge door. I finally decided to break off a tiny bit and eat it, but when I did the lollipop broke into a million pieces, with only a triangle left stuck to the stick. I left the triangle for her and ate up all the little pieces. As soon as she woke up, I hid.

When she saw what was left of her candy, Layla howled with rage. I'd never seen her that angry. She came after me like a bull after a red cape. I ran to my mother. Instead of scolding me, my mother told her that she shouldn't mind, and that as the big sister she should share her lollipop. I went to the fridge and brought her that skimpy little triangle, but Layla hurled it across the room. With no pride I scrambled across the floor, picked it up and ate it. Boy, was I mean. And to make matters worse, when the other kids found out she'd had to take me along, she wasn't invited to anymore birthday parties for a long, long time.

Layla said, "The way you ate my lollipop proves that you're selfish."

"But that was eight years ago. I was only five years old."

"Yeah, but you haven't changed. Yesterday you finished up all the juice. You didn't leave even a drop for anyone else. You only think about yourself."

"But there was only half a glass left."

"That doesn't matter. You should still have asked if anyone else wanted some instead of thinking only of yourself."

I didn't say anything. Maybe she was right. Maybe I was selfish.

Softly, Layla said, "I'm only telling you this for your own good. I don't want anyone thinking that my sister is selfish."

"But if I'm being selfish, why didn't Ami and Abi say anything?"

"They're not with you as much as I am and they don't know you like I do. Ami and Abi are good but they know the Pakistani ways. We're not in Pakistan anymore." She paused, letting that fact sink in a moment before continuing. "You don't know how lucky you are. I've always wished I had an older sister to tell me how to behave. It would have made things a lot easier for me. You're so lucky you've got me to tell you what you're doing wrong. I won't let you make the mistakes that I made."

Was it true? Did I only think of myself?

Layla continued, "We shouldn't be selfish like the way you were with the juice. We should be like those early Muslims. Remember the three men who were dying on the battlefield? The water carrier came to the first one to give him a drink, but the man, even though he was dying, said to go to his fellow Muslim first. Then the second man heard a third Muslim crying out for water, and told the carrier to give him a drink first. When the carrier went to the third man, he was already dead, so he went back to the second man and he was dead too. And so was the first one. We should be like that. Always thinking of others before ourselves."

That story always made me cry. I was crying now. Quietly, pushing my face into my pillow so Layla wouldn't hear. She was right. I was selfish. If I had been on that battlefield, I would've drunk the water first. I'd try to do better.

7

I stood at the head of the street where Jenny lived,
listening to the wind moan. The houses looked tired,
the paint peeling off the eavestroughs and cracking on
the wooden sidings. I'd already been waiting ten minutes and there were only ten minutes left till school
began, where was she?

I could hear screaming, faint and muted, coming
from one of the houses. I couldn't make out the words.
Every now and then there were quiet pauses, when the
listener must have been responding.

The wind blew up again, hostile, bitter, spraying
me with dust and fine gravel. I took the hint and left.
I'd have to see Jenny at school. I hoped she still wanted
to be my assistant.

By the time I got there, the bell had rung. I hurried to class. All the kids had settled down. Jenny was nowhere to be seen. I wondered if she was sick.

Mr. Weiss had just started his lesson when Jenny knocked timidly on the door. She handed him a late slip and marched to the back of the room, fumbling with the hangers in the coat closet. I snuck a look back at her. Her hair hung over her face, as usual, and she was careful to keep it there when she turned her head and knelt to pick up her jacket after it fell. Even so, I caught glimpses of her face beneath the veil. Her eyelids were red and swollen, and the tip of her nose was pink.

I glanced at Kevin. He hadn't seen Jenny come in. He was too busy talking to Cheryl.

Jenny hunched down behind the pages of her history textbook. By recess, she'd allowed some of her hair to fall back behind her ear. She gave me a watery smile when I came up to her. I resisted the urge to ask if she was all right. When I've been crying, that's the worse thing someone can do. Asking me if I'm all right just reminds me of why I was upset in the first place, and the tears, still fresh in my eyes, start to flow again.

I said, "So, do you still want to be my assistant?"

She gave me a genuine grin. "Sure."

I took her down by the gym and showed her the tryout sheets I'd posted the day before. "We'll hold auditions tomorrow."

She scratched at a pimple on her cheek while reading through the posted sheets. "Have you seen this?"

She pointed to the sheet marked Emperor. I expected the most number of names on it. There was only one, if you didn't count those that had been crossed out. In bold letters, twice the size of any other name on the page, was written Kevin with a big exclamation mark after it.

I said, "I can't believe it. How could he do such a stupid thing? I was going to make him Emperor, anyway."

She tossed the hair out of her eyes. "He won't be easy to work with."

"Neither will I, but I'm the director. He'll have to listen to me or get out."

Jenny glanced at me. "I don't know if, I mean, maybe that's not such a good way to handle him. I mean, he is the most popular kid in the school."

I giggled. "You know, when Mr. Weiss first gave me this assignment I pictured myself as the director, in the third row of a dark theatre, in a plush seat, the kind that flips up when you're not sitting on it, watching Kevin squirm under the hot stage lights and telling him to relax and take it from the top."

I giggled again. Jenny didn't. She bit her lip, frowning. I felt suddenly embarrassed. Maybe I shouldn't have told her that. It made me look as if I was on a power trip.

Jenny pointed to the next tryout sheet. "Did you see that one?"

It was the one marked Queen. Again there were a whole bunch of crossed-out names, and in the same bold hand was written Cheryl. I checked the sheet for Tailor 1, and Tailor 2, and Chamberlain. They were the same. Some of the names had been written in black ink, some in blue, some in a large scrawl, some in tiny letters in a slanted backhand, but they were all crossed out with the same bold stroke, using the same black ink. And at the bottom of each sheet was written a name, twice as large as all the others, in the same black ink. The nerve of Kevin. How dare he!

Quietly, Jenny said, "He's picked the cast for you."

"I know that!"

She brushed the hair away from her face. Her eyes looked angry. "You needn't bite my head off."

"I'm sorry. I'm really sorry," I muttered.

She turned away. "It's okay." The hair fell back into her eyes. "What are you going to do?"

"He won't get away with this." I marched up to the staff room and knocked on the door. Jenny tagged along. I asked for Mr. Weiss and when he appeared I thrust the tryout sheets at him, my voice trembling with rage. "Look, sir, look what he's done."

He leafed through the sheets, his bushy eyebrows drawn low over his eyes. When he finished, he puffed out his cheeks and let out a sigh. "That's too bad, Zainab. Who do you suppose did this?"

"Kevin, of course."

"What are you going to do about it?"

Me? He expected me to handle this? "Can't you make him stop?"

He frowned. "How?"

"I don't know. Talk to him, tell him to listen to me."

Mr. Weiss gave one backward glance, stepped into the hallway and closed the door behind him. He turned to Jenny. "Could you excuse us please, Jenny?"

Jenny's face was hidden. She was leaning against the wall, cradling her breasts on her folded arms. She nodded and walked away, looking back over her shoulder at me a couple of times as she went down the hall.

He said, "What do you suppose would happen if I talked to him?"

"He'd listen."

Mr. Weiss frowned, his bushy eyebrows bunching up in a mass. "Let me put it another way. Mackenzie King is winning in track and field, right?"

I nodded.

"What if they weren't? Could I go out and make some of the kids in Mackenzie King participate when they didn't want to?"

I pointed to the tryout sheets. "But, sir, he's preventing others from participating. That's not fair."

"I'm not allowed to get involved in the house league play. If you need props, materials, that kind of thing, I can help. Other than that, I'm afraid my hands are tied."

"But, sir, you could talk to him. Tell him to stop."

"I probably could but . . ." He drew in a sharp breath and leaned against the side of the door frame. "I knew it wouldn't be easy for you. I think you can handle this. If I didn't, I wouldn't have given you the job."

I felt like I was floating in mid-air, with nothing to cling to. "But, sir," I stammered. "I thought you were on my side."

"Oh, I am. That's why I won't interfere. The whole idea of your doing the play is to show them you're just as good as they are. How can you do that if I'm standing behind you making them listen?"

"But . . ." I couldn't think of anything to say.

He patted me on the shoulder. "Zainab, you don't know how tempting it is for me to step in and solve your problems."

His pants were falling down. He paused to pull them up and tuck in his shirt. "But that wouldn't be helping you. There are some things you just have to learn by yourself. This is one of them."

He sighed. "I won't always be around to make sure Kevin and those guys treat you fairly. This is a way for you to learn while still protected. Do you see why I have to let you deal with this on your own?"

"But he's trying to take over and it's my play."

"Yes, it is. That's one thing Kevin or anyone else can't take from you. It still is your play. You can still cast whomever you want."

I examined the speckled pattern of the hallway floor. Mr. Weiss ducked down to catch my eye. "Does that help?"

"Yeah, sure."

I turned and started down the hallway. By the time I got outside, there was only five minutes left of recess. Jenny was waiting. Icy blasts of wind snatched my breath away. Clouds were rolling in. It would snow in a few days. Jenny and I huddled in a corner by a window, trying to find shelter.

"What did Mr. Weiss say?"

"I'm on my own."

Jenny looked relieved. "So what are you going to do now?"

"After recess, I'm going to make an announcement

that the auditions are open to anyone who's interested. All they have to do is prove they can act. I'll pick only the best."

"That's a good idea."

I shrugged. "Maybe."

Kevin was out on the field, oblivious to the cold, playing football with his friends. His harem had turned into cheerleaders, their hair whipping around their reddened faces. Kevin intercepted a long pass, running down the field with hardly any resistance. Nobody dared tackle him.

Jenny glanced at me. "Have you ever been kissed by a boy?"

I was leaning against the muddy yellow school wall. My knees buckled, and I nearly fell. "What?"

Jenny cleared the hair from her face and met my startled gaze. "Have you ever been kissed by a boy?"

"Does my father or brother count?"

"No."

"Then, no."

She sighed. "Neither have I." The pimples on her chin had formed scabs. She scratched them off, leaving flecks of fresh blood that would form new scabs.

"But what about Kevin? I thought you two were, you know."

"We are. But he won't kiss me." She continued, "I just can't understand it. Why won't he? He says he loves me."

"Why don't you ask him?"

She looked at me alarmed. "Oh, no. He might get angry and leave."

"So what? You don't need him."

Her eyes were wide. "Oh, but I do . . . I love him."

She had such a dreamy look on her face, as the wind swirled her hair around her head, hiding her face, then revealing it again. Her eyes gazed off into the distance at something far away and invisible to me. For a moment, I have to admit, I was jealous. I remembered Mr. Rochester in *Jane Eyre*. He was the closest I'd ever come to being in love. But he only lived in a book.

After another long silence she said, "I keep telling him all I want is a little cuddling and some kissing, but he always wants more."

"You didn't give in, did you?" I blurted out, then stopped myself. I sounded like a mother.

She looked away. "Not yet."

Kevin made his touchdown. He raised his arms and strutted like a champion, spiking the ball into the frozen turf. His harem abandoned their cheerleading post, and mobbed him.

My father would have my head on a platter if I ever had a boyfriend. But then, no boy had shown an interest in me that way. I'd never been allowed to go to any of the school dances and, even if I had gone, white boys just weren't interested in brown girls. Premini Gupta didn't have a boyfriend either.

Jenny sighed, hanging her head so her hair fell over her face again.

The bell rang, and we filed slowly back inside.

8

It was not a plush theatre seat, but one of the cheap wooden chairs whose legs wobbled and groaned when you dragged them over the varnished wood floor of the gymnasium, and whose raw splintery edges snagged the threads of polyester pants. And I wasn't sitting in any third row in comfortable darkness while the actors on stage sweated under the hot stage lights. But I was in charge. All the hopeful would-be actors stood outside the gym doors, waiting to try out for their roles in my production. It was me they had to please.

There must be quite a few of them, I thought. There were faces pressed against the glass windows of the doors. Jenny squeezed through and came to look over my shoulder. I had the rough draft of the play on a clipboard. The top page was the cast of characters, with blanks to be filled in beside each name.

I said, "How many kids are waiting to try out?"

"Um, you could say there's a crowd." She looked away, avoiding my eyes.

"How many, exactly?"

"Three."

"Three! Aren't Kevin and his gang here yet?"

She shook her head, her hair swishing back and forth with the motion.

Darn! How could we start auditions with only three people? And yet we were fifteen minutes late already. "Send them in, Jenny. We might as well begin."

She nodded and was about to leave when she turned back instead. "Do you mind if I ask you something, Zainab?"

"Sure."

"Um, maybe I shouldn't. I mean, maybe it's none of my business, but what do you have against Premini Gupta?"

My back went rigid. "What makes you think I have something against her?"

"I got this feeling you did. I may be wrong, but . . ."

I began doodling in the margin of the top sheet — a witch with bulging eyes and a hooked nose. I said, "Why do you ask?"

"She's one of the crowd. I hope you'll be fair to her."

I scowled. "Of course I'll be fair." I put a few warts on the chin and nose of the witch. I have to admit I'd disliked Premini from the moment I saw her. When she first came to our class, even Mr. Weiss looked from her to me and expected us to be friends. Just because her parents happened to come from the same part of the world as mine, we were supposed to stick together? It put me off. But eventually I thought it was stupid to balk at being friends with her just because it was the expected thing. So I'd approached her.

She'd been sitting on a sofa in the reading area of the library, her nose in this huge book. She looked up and saw me watching her. She smiled. I smiled back and sat down. We talked about the books we loved, and it turned out we actually had a lot in common. We both loved *Anne of Green Gables*.

After an awkward silence, she gave a little cough and said, "Do you mind if I ask you a question?"

"What?"

"Do you eat eggs and meat?"

"Yes."

She looked me in the eye. "How could you? You're killing cute little baby chicks and animals that haven't done anything to you."

The question and her accusing tone threw me off-kilter. I didn't know what to say. I could feel the hot flush creeping up my face to the roots of my hair.

She was looking at me smugly. Not really expecting me to answer. She obviously thought she was much better than me. I got up and walked away. There was no way we'd ever be friends.

Jenny tapped my shoulder. "Ready?"

I nodded. They were banging on the doors.

Premini Gupta was the first through. Her Lucky jeans were still new and so tight and stiff she walked as if she was made of cardboard. The other two members of the "crowd" were the class geometry champions — Fran, a skinny bucktoothed girl with glasses, and Dan, a skinny bucktoothed boy with glasses. They could have been twins, except Fran had red hair and Dan had brown.

I looked us over. Jenny, me, Premini and the geometry twins. The bottom of the class barrel. Was it enough to put on the play? Maybe, barely, if we all, including Jenny, took a part and doubled-up on the backstage duties.

But where was Kevin? Without him, no one would take us seriously. And without him, how would Mackenzie King ever win? How would Kevin and all the other kids in the class get to know me? How would they realize I wasn't so bad? Questions buzzed through my head, like the low hum of the fluorescent lights, leaving my throat dry and my forehead beaded with sweat.

I stood up, clutching the clipboard so tight my knuckles hurt. I took a deep breath, and lied as best I could, "I don't care how many people we have in our play, I just care that everyone tries his or her best. We'll begin auditions and if anyone comes late they'll have to wait their turn. To audition you can recite a poem, act a part in a play you've seen or play one of the roles in your favorite T.V. show. All I'm trying to see is who are the best actors. The best actors will get the speaking parts and, if there's anyone left, they'll either be in the crowd when the emperor wears his new clothes, or help backstage. Okay, who'd like to go first?"

They shuffled their feet and looked at each other,

suddenly shy. No one stepped forward. I sat down, looking them over, like a teacher. There were only three of them, but still the feeling of power tingled through my veins. It was the first time in my life that I'd ever felt it. My eye rested on Premini Gupta.

I had a score to settle with her. What better way than by making her go first?

When I called her name, she stood up straight. "Me?"

I nodded.

She came to the middle of the gymnasium and in a soft voice that cracked a bit when she first spoke, said, "I'm going to do Shylock's speech from Shakespeare's *The Merchant of Venice*."

We'd studied *The Merchant of Venice* in English the year before. I'd liked Shylock's speech, too.

Before our eyes, Premini's face changed. She stood a little stooped over, as if holding a cane, as if she really were a middle-aged man speaking his thoughts. Sneering at an imaginary Antonio, talking to us as if he really were her mortal enemy, making us see that a Jew was a person like ourselves, even though she was not a Jew but a Hindu. She was good. I had to admit it. She made me forget I was in a bright gymnasium, with fluorescent lamps shining their sickly light down on me. She held all of us spellbound. No feet shuffled. Nobody moved at all.

When she was done, she was trembling. Her forehead shone damp, and sweat dotted her upper lip. Nobody said a word for a long moment. Fran started clapping tentatively, but somehow it seemed wrong to disturb the power of the performance with such a noisy form of approval.

I had no choice. In all fairness, I had to write her name down in the queen's space. She was good enough to play the emperor but she'd have to settle for Queen.

"Who's next?" I called. The kids in line backed away. Nobody wanted to follow that performance. I didn't blame them.

Then Kevin and two-thirds of the class barged in.

A noisy, boisterous crowd. We gawked at them. I said to Kevin, loud enough to be heard over the racket, "You're late."

Kevin shrugged. "So what? We're here now and we're ready to audition."

"Not so fast!" I turned to the geometry twins. "Who wants to go next?"

They glanced from Kevin to me. Nobody volunteered. Jenny bent and whispered in my ear, "You might as well let them go first."

I nodded. "Okay, Kevin, you're on."

I was expecting to be impressed. After all, he was the only one in the whole school who was a professional actor.

He took his jacket off and draped it over his shoulders. Then with one hand resting haughtily on his hip, and the other poised in the air as if holding a royal sceptor, he strutted around the gym with his nose in the air. He did this for two minutes. I know because I timed him. The five of us who'd seen Premini's performance were quiet. Kevin's gang cheered and laughed at every gesture, every regal nod of the head and change of expression.

When he was finally finished, I asked, "And what are you supposed to be?"

His face turned red and his frosty blue eyes nailed me with venom. "The emperor, who else?"

I shrugged. "Wasn't sure."

I kept my eyes on the clipboard, jotting down Kevin's name in the blank beside the word Emperor. The scratch of my pen and the hum of the fluorescent lights were the only sounds in the whole gym. All eyes were glued to us, I could feel them. I just knew that if I said anything, anything at all, Kevin would pounce on me like a wolf.

Somebody coughed. Somehow it was enough to break the tension. The moment had passed. I could speak again. I looked up. Kevin had moved back within his group. "Who's next?"

He nudged Cheryl forward. She glanced uncertainly back at Kevin. He nodded. Turning back, she gave me a simpering smile. Then she curtsied in an old-fashioned way, and started prancing around in a circle, twirling and lifting imaginary skirts. She stopped in front of me.

"And what are you supposed to be?"

She frowned and looked back again at Kevin. When he nodded once more, she turned back to me and said, "Uh, the queen."

There were a few quickly smothered snickers. I gave a little shrug, and Cheryl went back to Kevin's side. Jenny whispered in my ear, "You won't write her name down, will you?"

"I have to Jenny, but she'll just be in the crowd."

I don't know how I sat through all those auditions. Almost everyone either copied Kevin's saunter or Cheryl's prancing. There were a few though, in Kevin's group, who were good enough to play the tailors and the chamberlain.

"Okay," said Kevin, when the last person had auditioned. "Who's who?"

I said, "Ahem, I haven't quite made up my mind. I've prepared an excercise that real actors do to help them concentrate. We don't want anyone to start laughing in the middle of their lines."

Kevin looked annoyed, but allowed me to continue. "Everybody get a partner, make a pair," I said.

Kevin picked Cheryl. There were too many girls and not enough boys. "It's okay," I called. "Girls can be partners in this."

Kevin said something rude, but luckily it wasn't loud enough for me to have to deal with it.

In the end, Premini didn't have a partner. She stood aloof, and looking cool. Not upset, like I would have been. I didn't want to do it, but for the sake of the play, I said, "I'll be your partner, Premini."

She gave me a smile and walked over.

My hands were sweaty. I hoped the book I'd read was right. But it was too late now. It had to be right. I raised my voice so everyone would hear over their chatter. "Okay, now one of you has to say this line to your partner and your partner has to reply but without smiling. This is to see if you can keep a straight face."

"Oh, brother," said Kevin. "Where'd you get this, Zainy?"

I ignored him. "Now the one person has to say, 'Darling, if you love me, would you please, please smile?'"

"What?" cried Kevin. "What's so funny about that?"

There were a lot of snickers. And it took a while to restore peace.

I clenched my fists and continued to ignore Kevin. "Now the other person can't smile, but must reply, 'Darling, you know I love you but I just can't smile.'"

Then I took out the prize. I held up a chocolate bar and said, "Whoever can do it without smiling gets this. You can't touch the other person, but you can make funny faces while you're saying it."

Suddenly everyone was serious. I wasn't that worried. According to the book, this was a very difficult exercise. I'd probably get to keep my chocolate bar. Judging from all the laughter, the book was right.

I turned to Premini. Her eyes were narrowed, and she looked smug. It was as if I could read her mind, or maybe it was her expression. She believed that chocolate bar was hers.

"Which one do you want to be?" I asked.

"You say it to me and I won't smile."

"Okay." I licked my lips. Just thinking about it made me smile, but it didn't matter. I wasn't the one who had to keep a straight face. "Darling . . ." I fluttered my eyelashes, and clasped my hands. ". . . if you love me, would you please, please smile?"

I swear, it was as if her face was carved of stone. She looked at me like I was a fly on the wall. And calmly, without a hint of a smile said, "Darling, you know I love you but I just can't smile."

It couldn't be that easy. I'd be in trouble if it was. The book said no beginner could do it. What if everyone thought it was that easy? I only had one chocolate bar. They'd be furious. I said, "Okay, you do it to me."

She nodded. Premini crossed her eyes and wrinkled her nose and made fishy lips. Looking deep into my eyes, she said in a soft passionate voice (not easy with fishy lips), "Dahling, if you luv me . . ."

I burst out laughing.

The group was getting chaotic. Shrieks of laughter, and Kevin was tickling Cheryl.

"Okay, okay everyone. Who can do it?"

Two hands went up. Premini's and Kevin's.

"Well," I said. "I only have one chocolate bar. You do it to each other and whoever doesn't smile, wins it."

Kevin went first, though it was clear he found Premini repugnant. "Darling . . ." He snorted like a pig, and puckered his lips, making kissy noises. Premini crossed her arms and watched him impassively. Everyone else was laughing at Kevin's antics, including Kevin. "Darling, if you love me, would you please, please . . ." Here he jumped around like a gorilla and scratched his armpit. Premini remained unmoved. "Darling, if you love me, would you please, please smile?"

With a calm straight face, Premini said, "Darling, you know I love you but I just can't smile."

Kevin scowled. Now it was his turn. In a calm husky voice, she looked straight into Kevin's eyes and said, "Dahling, if you luv me, would you please —"

Kevin burst out laughing. But was so furious he knocked his books off his chair.

Premini collected her chocolate bar. She was definitely good enough to be Emperor.

When everyone had settled down, I stood up and read my decision. "The emperor will be played by Kevin, the queen by Premini, the chamberlain by Bill, the —" I got no further.

Kevin roared, "What! There's no way Premini's going to be my queen."

Jenny squeezed my arm in warning. I didn't need it. I stood up, calmly, but my breath came in shallow gasps, as if I'd run ten laps. I couldn't afford to let Kevin walk out those doors, and yet Premini deserved the part. In a calm voice, I said, "Kevin, you are the star. You're the emperor. You got what you wanted. To be fair, I have to give the part of the queen to the best actress. It happens to be Premini."

Kevin clenched his jaw and pointed at Premini. "There's no way I'll have that as my queen."

My hands were so sweaty the clipboard slipped in my grasp. I clutched it tighter, and said again, "Premini got the part, fair and square. I'm just trying to make Mackenzie King win. To do that, I have to choose the best person for the part."

Kevin bared his teeth, wrinkling his nose. He looked at me like I was a mouse in his path, like he was deciding whether to swallow me whole or chew me up into little pieces. He said, "I don't know why Weiss gave you the play. We'll never win with you directing it, anyway. If you don't make Cheryl Queen, then I won't play Emperor."

The clipboard slipped from my fingers and fell to the gym floor with a loud clatter. All heads turned to me. I looked straight into the terrifying eyes of the wolf and took a deep breath. "In that case, Kevin, you won't be Emperor."

Kevin's lip curled. "In that case, " he mimicked, "you'll have no play. Everyone out."

With his nose in the air, and his jacket still draped over his shoulders, he sauntered out the door followed by all but three of the kids — Premini and the geometry twins.

The clipboard was still on the floor. The rough draft of the play lay in a scattered heap and my pen lay buried somewhere beneath it. I was numb, staring at the mess without really seeing it. Premini marched up to me. She cleared her throat and I looked up in a daze.

Wrinkling her nose, she said, "What makes you think I even wanted to be the queen? I should have been the emperor!"

She turned and marched out too.

9

It was chilly in the rec room and dark. Outside, the sky was bleak and dreary. A steady drizzle was falling and soon the sun would set. The tiny windows just under the basement ceiling let in little light, and what light that did enter was quickly eaten by the dark wood paneling of the walls. I sat there in the gloom, chewing my lip, wondering what on earth I was going to do about the play.

I'd got home after the rehearsal and let myself in silently. Like a thief, I'd crept downstairs, turned on the tap so it trickled quietly, made wudu and prayed. Layla was somewhere upstairs, torturing the twins by the sounds of it. The house had the hostile feeling it held whenever my parents weren't home. As long as

Layla wasn't aware of my presence, she wouldn't be bugging me.

I bit my lip so hard I drew blood. It tasted like a tin can. Layla was calling me. She must have heard me come in. I didn't answer. She barged into the rec room, didn't see me right away and left, grumbling about how late I was, how lazy, how she had to do all the work around here, and how she'd tell Ami how late I was. A moment later she returned, peering into the gloom, then turning on the light to be sure. The sudden brightness was blinding.

"Shut that thing off!" I cried, shielding my eyes. And before she could nag at me, "Assalaamu alaikum."

"Why are you sitting in the dark? Have you prayed yet? Prayer time is going."

"Yes, I prayed. I was just thinking."

She cocked her head, her long black ponytail swishing to fall down the side of her neck. "Thinking? Of what? What's the matter? You've been awfully quiet these days."

I was tempted to tell her. Why not? The worst she could do was give me advice I couldn't use. Ultimately it was up to me. "It's about the play."

She sat down on the coffee table, leaning forward, her eyes aglow with interest. "Yes? Are you doing a hadith?"

"No! I'm doing *The Emperor's New Clothes*."

"You really should do a hadith."

I kept the growl out of my voice; there was no way I could afford to "disrespect" her. "No, not a hadith. *The Emperor's New Clothes*. Anyway, there's this guy, the most popular kid in the whole school . . ."

I told her how Kevin had turned the whole class against the play and that without him I couldn't put it on. When I was finished, she nodded. "Oh, dear. It sounds like you're really in a jam."

"Yep. What should I do?"

Layla cleared her throat and shifted in her seat. "Gee, I don't know. I don't think I should get involved. After all, it's your play. You're probably not going to listen to my advice anyway. You didn't listen when I told you to do a hadith."

"I just didn't think the other kids would like a hadith."

Layla patted my hand. "You go right ahead and think that if you want to. No one's going to stop you. Least of all me."

"But don't you have any suggestions as to what I could do?"

Layla grimaced. "You're not going to like them. I'd better just keep them to myself."

"But what are they? Tell me."

"Are you sure?"

"Yes. Please!"

"Well then. I think you should humble yourself before Kevin. Beg his forgiveness. There's no way you can do the play without him. I thought it was strange when the teacher asked you, to begin with."

"What! Humiliate myself for the sake of a play!"

"Isn't that what you did to him?"

"Not really. He had it coming. He was expecting to pick the whole cast for me."

Layla frowned again.

"What?" I demanded.

"Nothing."

"No, tell me. What are you thinking?"

"Well, I'm just wondering what's wrong with him picking the cast?"

What was wrong with that? I couldn't believe she could be so dense. I already regretted my impulse to confide in her. I should've known she'd never understand.

Layla looked unhappy. "You know what your problem is?"

I held up my hand to stop her. "Wait a minute. I still have a few hours till it's time to list my faults."

She threw up her hands in frustration. "See? That's just my point. You're too darn arrogant to listen to anybody."

Arrogant? Now I was arrogant? Couldn't I do anything right? Didn't I even have the right to be upset?

Layla continued, "Your problem is that you're so arrogant you think you know it all, and you think you're better than everyone else — a deadly combination."

I thought of Premini and bit back my retort. Maybe I should listen.

She continued, "Whenever anyone has a suggestion that doesn't go along with yours, you just automatically toss it out the window. I suggested you do a hadith, use this opportunity to educate your classmates about the beauty of Islam, but did you listen? No. You just automatically tossed it out the window without even giving it proper consideration. Now this boy comes along and picks the cast for you — do you consider that he might have picked the right people? No. You humiliate him in front of all his friends and then wonder why he's so upset he just walks out of the play and takes everyone else with him.

"That's called arrogance. One of the worse sins you could ever commit. You do remember that it was arrogance that was the downfall of Pharoah? It was arrogance that made him think he was God. It was arrogance that made him defy the requests of Moses, peace be upon him. And here you are just as arrogant, expecting to defy everyone and get away with it."

I couldn't stay silent for another minute. "If Kevin had come and suggested these people, I would have considered them."

"Really?"

"Yes," I said.

"I made a suggestion. Did you consider it? I mean, seriously consider it?"

Maybe I had been quick to discard the idea of doing a hadith. Too quick?

Layla had her arms folded across her chest. "You do know I'm right, don't you? Look into the depths of your soul and see if you don't hate being wrong. If you're too arrogant to admit when you're wrong . . . well then, I feel sorry for you. Because then there really is no hope for your improvement. I might as well forget about those self-improvement sessions we've been having. Because until you conquer your arrogance you'll just be going in circles."

I stared at the palms of my empty hands, the words

"no hope for you" echoing over and over, like one of Premini's Hindu mantras, in my brain. I swallowed several times, watching the lines in the palms of my hands come in and out of focus, till I was sure I would sound normal, then said, "So what do you think I should do?"

Layla put a hand on my arm. I wanted to pull my arm away, but didn't.

Her voice was gentle, comforting. "The best way to fight arrogance is with humility. Go to Kevin. Humble yourself before him. Remember, Allah loves those who humble themselves."

I looked up, confused. "But Layla. The verse in the Quran says that Allah loves those who humble themselves before their Lord. Not before other people."

She thought for a moment. "Yes, but you were wrong. In this case, you have to humble yourself in front of the person you wronged. It will be hard, but believe me, it's the only way."

I wished my mother was home. I would have liked to ask her what she thought. Half an hour later she did come home. But she was too busy getting supper together to listen.

After we ate, I washed the dishes without being asked to. Layla inspected them and pronounced them clean, all except for three plates, two spoons, a saucer and a fork. I'd left a few traces of food on them. To show how "unarrogant" I could be, I thanked her for pointing out those dirty dishes to me.

My mother gave me a hug. "It's so nice to see you helping out more. You know, I was quite worried about you. You were getting quite selfish. Always hiding when there was work to be done. It's good to see you doing your share."

Beyond my mother's shoulder, Layla was nodding and smiling encouragingly, or was it triumphantly? It was hard to tell.

I released myself from my mother's arms and went to sweep the floor.

When Ami came to call me for school the next morning, I hid deeper within my cave of sheets and blankets. She asked if I was sick. No, I admitted. I just didn't want to go to school.

She asked why not.

It was such a long story. The auditions, Premini, Kevin, Dahling, you know I luv you but I just can't smile. Oh, geez. Rather than explain, I got up and got ready.

I had oatmeal for breakfast. It was lumpy and grey and looked the way I felt.

The night before, Layla had informed me that I was hard-hearted, stubborn, spiteful, moody, and I took too long in the shower. I knew I took too long in the shower, but those other things? I'd never thought I was like that until last night. She used lots of specific examples, events that I barely remembered. She gave me the time, the date, and the exact circumstances in which the fault was demonstrated. She should be a lawyer. The proof she gave me was overwhelming. I don't know how she did it. How could she remember something I did three months before? It was as if she'd filed it away in her brain to use sometime in the future against me.

And she always told me about faults I didn't know I had. She never mentioned the ones I was well aware of. If she'd told me that I favored some people over others, just because they were popular, so that some of their popularity would rub off on me, she'd have had a point. I wouldn't even have argued with her.

Though she did grant me one concession. "Selfishness" had been deleted, and replaced with "arrogance."

The ever-growing list of my faults was so long that I hadn't been able to get to sleep till past twelve. That's why I felt as dreary as my oatmeal in the morning. Layla sat across from me. She looked as sunny as the sky peeking through the kitchen window. Why should she look so rested, so satisfied, when I hadn't got a wink of sleep all night? My head ached and my oatmeal had gone cold.

I jumped at the knock on the door. It was Jenny.

10

I left the rest of my breakfast, grabbed my jacket and hurried out the door. The day was cold, the first snow of winter a thin layer on the ground. Blades of grass, still green and determined, poked through the gauzy white. Only a month till Christmas holidays. We should at least have begun rehearsals by then. But maybe the play was doomed.

"So how are you doing?" asked Jenny.

I shrugged. "Not too well, actually. How did you know where I lived?"

Jenny blushed. "Don't think I'm weird, but the first day of school, I followed you home. I wanted to talk to you. I wasn't spying, honest I wasn't."

I laughed. "You're kidding! I never guessed."

Jenny said, "Have you finished writing the play?"

"Almost. Maybe we could go somewhere to work on it. I wouldn't mind some help."

Jenny kicked a stone out of her way and shrugged. "How about your house?"

I'd hoped she'd suggest hers. I still didn't know exactly where she lived and my mother always told me it was rude to ask, like asking for an invitation. I said, "That's okay, but I better warn you. I share a room with my big sister and the twins are a pain in the neck."

"Twins! How sweet! Do they look the same?"

"No. One's a boy, one's a girl."

"I wish I had a brother or sister. In our house, it's just me and my mom."

Jenny glanced at me through her veil of hair. "I know it's none of my business . . . maybe I shouldn't even be asking. Don't get mad or anything . . . but what do you have against Premini?"

Not again. "Nothing! I have nothing against her!"

She gave me a hurt look. "I mean, at yesterday's rehearsal. You said you'd give the parts to whoever was the best."

I nodded.

"You're making her the queen. I'm not trying to tell you how to run the play, and I may be wrong, but I don't even remember a queen in the story. She can't have a very big part to play."

I'd never heard Jenny say so many words at one time.

"Is it because she's a girl? Is that why you didn't make her Emperor?"

"Yes it is! Now stop hassling me!"

Jenny hid behind her hair, pouting. "I thought you were different. That's all. I thought you were fair."

It wasn't easy being fair. I don't like to admit it, but Premini's accusation had bugged me more than I wanted it to. I'd always thought Islam was better than all other religions. But we did eat meat. We did kill cute little lambs and cows and chickens and eat them. I could picture Premini laughing. Thinking that being Hindu made her so much better than us. I tried to forget that I'd been doing the very same thing.

Pakistan was once a part of India, so we're both kind of Indian. But as a Muslim, I've always felt as though I have more in common with Christians and Jews than Hindus.

Jenny bit her lower lip.

"I'm sorry, Jenny. It's just that if I don't give Kevin the emperor, he won't be in the play."

Jenny put her hand on my arm. Even through my jacket it felt warm and comforting. "Are you sure that's the only reason? I really get the feeling you hate her."

"Okay. Maybe I do. You want to know why? Because she thinks she's so much better than me just because she doesn't eat eggs."

Jenny frowned. "I eat eggs."

"Premini said that when you eat eggs you're killing cute little baby chicks."

Jenny said, "That's not true. I used to live on a farm with my grandfather. I know."

"You mean you don't kill chicks when you eat eggs?"

"No. The eggs we eat don't have chicks in them. In order for there to be a chick inside, a rooster has to, um . . ."

A red flush crept up her face.

I came to her rescue. "You mean the eggs aren't fertilized?"

She heaved a sigh of relief. "Yes."

"But what about the meat?"

Jenny shrugged. "Well, yeah." Then she frowned. "It's funny that Premini only asked you about that. Everyone else in the class eats meat too and she's never asked us."

"See? She picked on me first. Why should I like her?"

Jenny chewed her lip, kicking a stone out of her way. "Well, maybe you don't have to like her. But, I mean, don't you think you should be fair?"

"If I'm fair, Kevin will leave and take all the kids with him."

"Not all the kids."

"Jenny! Only three kids showed up on their own. And they were the only ones who stayed after Kevin left. That's just not enough!"

"You could do a different play. We don't have to do *The Emperor's New Clothes*."

"Like what?"

"Don't you have something, you know? A good story from your culture? There must be something. Honestly, I think the teachers judging the competition would really like something different."

Through gritted teeth I said, "There's no way I'm

going to do a story from my culture. I am not, I repeat, not going to give Kevin more stuff to make fun of me with!"

We walked for a long time in silence. The snow melting as the sun climbed higher, gaining strength. Jenny broke the silence. "What if Premini plays the emperor? We could probably talk some of the Mackenzie King kids into taking the other parts."

I'd thought about that too. But I didn't like the idea. I guess it was mean of me, but I knew the only people we'd get would be the losers, the nobodies, and I already had two of them — the geometry twins. The whole idea of the play was for Kevin and the popular kids to get to know me, and hopefully, to like me. How would that happen if they weren't a part of the play? Besides, I did want to win. They'd like me if we won.

Jenny interrupted my thoughts. "Well? Are you going to talk to Premini?"

"Well, yeah, I'm going to tell her I'm choosing Kevin. Then I'm going to talk to Kevin. I'll let Cheryl be the queen, it isn't a big part anyway. I'll just warn him that he has to be at rehearsals on time and listen to me, I'm still the director."

Jenny shook her head. "I don't think that's going to work. There's no way he's going to listen to you. And that Cheryl really is a twit. I can't imagine what Kevin sees in her."

She'd pushed her hair behind her ears and stared ahead.

We were just passing her street when a thought

occurred to me. "Did you finish your lab assignment?"

Jenny bit her lip. "Oh my gosh. I forgot it at home. Thanks so much."

We ran down her street. Hers was the last house. The one right beside the railway line. Painted a faded blue and yellow, the screen on the screen door had a huge hole in it. The ragged ends of the wire mesh twisted outward, as if a fist had gone through it.

She said, "Come on in. Don't mind the mess. I didn't get time to wash up before I called on you. Oh, you don't have to take your shoes off. Just wait in the kitchen while I run in."

A shrill voice yelled, "Jenny! Is that you?"

Jenny frowned at me. "Mandy? You're home? I thought you'd have left for work by now."

A skinny girl (lady?) wearing a short red skirt and a navy blue striped T-shirt with a sailor's collar skipped into the room.

"I thought you didn't have a sister, Jenny," I said.

The girl blushed and giggled. "I'm not her sister, you dear little thing, I'm her mother. But thanks for the compliment."

She had a nest of dirty blonde hair piled loosely on her head. A lit cigarette dangled from the corner of her mouth. She took a drag and bent to peer at her reflection in the grubby toaster. She added a dab of mascara.

Jenny looked from her mother to me. "Uh, Mandy, this is Zainab . . . from school. Zainab, this is my mother."

I tried not to stare. "Good morning, Mrs. Roberts."

She grinned. "That's Ms. Roberts, but soon to be

Mrs. if all goes well, eh, Jenny?" She winked at Jenny. Jenny rolled her eyes and went down the hall.

Ms. Roberts poured a cup of black coffee and gulped it down, quite noisily. She smiled at me. "I'm so nervous, I'm shaking. Look." She held out her hand and it was indeed trembling.

I felt compelled to ask. "Why are you so nervous, Ms. Roberts?"

She waved her red lacquered nails at me. "Oh, call me Mandy! Ms. Roberts sounds so old! As for why I'm so nervous . . ." She raised her voice and aimed it at the hallway so Jenny could hear too. "I think he's going to pop the question today, Jen. Oooh, I know he is. He called me up and told me to get all dolled up, he's taking me for lunch, and he has something very important to say. Oooh, I just know it. I'm getting married."

Jenny's voice carried out to us, in the kitchen. "I thought you were going to work today."

Ms. Roberts, Mandy, was looking into a compact and touching up her lipstick. She gave a smack and closed the compact with a click. "By tonight, I may never need to work again."

Jenny came rushing out, clutching her wrinkled assignment triumphantly. "Found it. Come on, Zainab."

"Wish me luck!" called Mandy.

"Good luck," I said.

Jenny didn't answer.

11

When I got to class, I felt like I was under a microscope. Everyone watched every move I made, ready to pounce. Kevin glared at me. I could feel his eyes on the back of my neck when I was sitting in class — I always sat near the front, and he and the cool guys sat at the back. But whenever I turned around to look, he was flirting with Cheryl.

At least once we got in class, Jenny seemed too wrapped up in Kevin and Cheryl's flirting to bother me about being fair to Premini. For that I was thankful. She sat hunched over in her seat, her hair falling in her face, her arms crossed, cradling her breasts.

Premini watched me like a tiger in the woods. I avoided her eye.

Mr. Weiss too, seemed to be watching me. One eyebrow raised, like a black caterpillar doing pushups.

Toward the end of the day, Mr. Weiss asked for volunteers to clean the chalkboards and dust the erasers. No one volunteered, so he picked me and Premini. Just my luck.

As soon as the class left, I grabbed the chalkboard erasers and went outside to bang them together. Great clouds of white dust tickled my nose and powdered my clothes, but it felt good to be pounding them like that. Harder and harder, till the erasers were quite flattened and no more dust escaped.

I went back upstairs to find that Premini had taken a chamois and washed down the blackboards and ledges.

She glanced at me as I came in. We were alone. Mr. Weiss was down at the office. She said, "I want to know what you've decided about the play. Is it me or Kevin?"

I was surprised she'd just come out with it like that. Surprised and a little impressed.

"Um, I've decided on Kevin."

She nodded, her mouth a bitter line. "I thought so."

I should have left it at that. I didn't owe her any explanations. But before I knew it, they were gushing out of my mouth anyway, like a dam had broken. "It's just that without Kevin half the class won't be in the play. You're real good. Honest, you are. It's just that I need Kevin and the others because we can't win on our own. Without Kevin none of the others will come along. You saw there were only five of us. How can we put on a play with only five people? And besides, this is supposed to represent all of Mackenzie King, not just a handful."

Premini interrupted. "They're not going to accept you, you know."

I stopped in my tracks.

"What are you talking about?"

Premini looked at me out of narrowed eyes. She looked like a cat. A self-satisfied Indian cat with a secret. "You think if you include Kevin and all those white kids in your play they'll let you into their exclusive little group. Well, I'm telling you it's not going to work."

"I don't know what you're talking about," I said, and started straightening some desks.

"Don't even try to lie. You're not the actress, remember? I am."

Premini wore a look of regal authority, almost like within her she knew exactly the tone of voice and expression that a king would use. A king who expected very much to be obeyed. It was as if she really was an emperor and I her subject. Standing on a chair towering over me as she wiped the board only added to the effect. I didn't dare cross her. I just stood there and listened.

"The way I see it, all whites are the same. They'll never accept you. They don't think we're as smart as them. Of course we are. Smarter even. And we have to be, to beat them at their own game. Then they might respect us, but still they'll never accept us."

"How can you say all whites are the same? What about Mr. Weiss? What about Jenny?"

Premini thought for a moment. "Mr. Weiss doesn't count. He can afford to be nice to us because we're kids, and not threatening to his status quo."

"Status quo?"

She rolled her eyes and sighed. "We're not on his level. He can afford to be nice. It's the same with Jenny. She's white trash. We're better than her so she has to be nice to us. Doesn't mean she'd accept us if she were in with Kevin's group."

"Jenny's not like that."

Premini laughed. "Don't you see she's chasing after Kevin just as much as you are? She wants the same thing, to be accepted. But in that she might be ahead of us. She's got something he wants."

"What do you mean?"

Premini gave me a *You just don't get it, do you?* look, opened her mouth as if to explain, then shook her head. "Never mind. She's as anxious to please Kevin as you are. And if she gets in with his crowd, you can bet she'll dump you at the first word from him."

"She would not."

Premini shrugged. "Think what you like. We'll see."

"You're saying all whites are the same. That's prejudice. Have you met all the whites? How can you say that?"

"Look, Zainab. I'm only trying to help. If you don't want my help, if you think you can handle it on your own, you're welcome to. But don't say I didn't warn you."

She'd finished washing the blackboard, and jumped off the chair. In another moment she'd be out the door and our chance at being friends would be gone. "Listen, Premini. Don't go away like that. I was hoping we could be friends."

She didn't meet my eyes. She played with the buckle on her school bag.

I said, "I may not agree with you, but I do think you're a terrific actor, and I wish you well."

Her look softened. "You really think I'm a good actor?"

I grinned. She was fishing for compliments. But heck, why not? She deserved them. "Yeah. You were a lot better than Kevin. I just wish I didn't have to choose."

She shrugged. "Actually, I'd probably do the same thing if I were director." She hesitated. "Mind if I ask you a question?"

"Go ahead."

"You're well-read. I mean to say, you read a lot. Why'd you pick *The Emperor's New Clothes*?

I guess she didn't expect an answer, because she didn't wait for one.

She continued, "I guess it's just as well, all this stuff with Kevin. To tell you the truth, I'm not crazy about the story you chose."

"But I thought you liked it. I thought you wanted to be the emperor."

Premini shook her head. "I want to be the star of the play, any play, not necessarily the emperor."

"Oh," I said, feeling rather foolish. Maybe Layla was right yet again. Maybe it was a babyish play to be doing.

Premini said, "Maybe you should do a Moghul story, something from India. Wouldn't that be fun? Bet those judges would like a break from the ordinary."

I couldn't believe it. Premini wanted me to do something "cultural" too!

I guess my disgust for her suggestion showed on my face. She took a quick look at me and said, "Fine. Fine. It's only a suggestion. Take it or leave it, as you wish. It's your play."

I smiled and nodded.

She said, "Are you finished up here? I'm heading off home."

I grabbed my books, and we walked down together to the big doors.

I asked her if she was going to be an actor when she grew up.

She laughed. "Naw. My parents want me to be a doctor. They'd flip if I told them I like acting." Premini grinned and twisted her face to look older and masculine. Wagging her finger in a stern way, she said with a thick Indian accent, "As loong as id doesn't inderfere in your school verk you can go to da play acting claass."

I laughed. She was so good.

At the end of the pavement, we parted.

As for Kevin, I didn't get a chance to speak to him until the next day. I was waiting to catch him alone but, weird, he was never alone. He always had someone, some guy hanging around, or some girl clutching onto him. Cheryl was sick, so Jenny was his girl for the day.

School was over, the bell had rung. I figured it was now or never, so I plucked up my courage and walked right up to him, as if I had every right to.

Kevin had his fingers hooked in the beltloops of

Jenny's Lucky jeans. A mini-leash of sorts. And he was joking around, whispering something in Jenny's ear, and laughing at the look of shock on her face. Laughing a loud throaty laugh, in a way that made Jenny squirm and me quite uncomfortable.

I don't know what I said, or maybe I just don't want to remember. Layla would have been proud though. Proud of the way I humbled myself before Kevin. She couldn't call me arrogant anymore. Perhaps I could cross that off my list of faults now.

The funny thing was, Kevin had decided Premini could go ahead and have the part. He wasn't interested anymore. I couldn't believe it. All that humbling for nothing. I just couldn't let him get away. I begged and begged, with real tears in my eyes. I told him how much I, we, Mackenzie King needed him. Without him we'd never win the competition.

I watched his face harden into a mask. He crossed his arms. He looked more and more impatient with every passing minute. Glancing at the door and the clock.

Even I could hear the note of desperation creeping into my voice. "Could you at least tell the others to come out?"

Kevin scowled. "Why would I do that?"

My entreaties were falling on deaf ears. All was lost till Jenny stepped up.

"I'd really appreciate it," said Jenny.

We both turned and stared at her.

Kevin had a calculating look on his face.

Wisps of hair covered her eyes again. She bit her

lip. "I mean, I really would appreciate it, Kevin. It would help Zainab out."

"Yeah?" said Kevin. "How much would you appreciate it?"

Jenny sighed. Her chest rose and fell. "A lot, Kevin. I'd appreciate it a lot."

Kevin said to me, though his eyes were still on Jenny, "You'll have to give Cheryl the part of the queen."

Jenny frowned, but I nodded.

"And all the other parts to my friends too."

"Of course."

Kevin smiled, and it was as if the sun came out and the ice in his eyes melted a little.

"Okay, I'll do it."

I clasped my hands like I'd seen the schoolmarms do in old westerns, when the hero was about to save the ranch. "So you're going to do it, Kevin? You're going to be our emperor?"

"Wait a minute," said Kevin. "I am kind of busy with football."

Jenny said, "But football only goes another week. Surely you could do it."

"Yeah, I guess so."

"We'll have the first reading tomorrow after school. And we'll start designing the sets and costumes."

Kevin shrugged. "Whatever."

He pulled Jenny into him, and put his arm around her shoulder, starting to steer her away. "How much did you say you'd appreciate it?"

I felt dismissed. Jenny did glance once over her shoulder with a little wave goodbye. I mouthed the word "Thanks." But I felt rather uneasy. Like something had happened that I wasn't aware of. Had Jenny given in to one of Kevin's demands? Nonsense, I told myself. I just couldn't believe my good luck.

With that done, I felt relieved. There was a bounce in my step as I went down the stairs and burst through the big doors.

I was looking forward to my list of faults that night. But when Layla started, arrogance was the first thing she mentioned. She'd decided to alphabetize the list, it made it easier to keep track. I objected, and told her about what had happened with Kevin. "Surely I'm not arrogant if I could humble myself before him," I said.

"Hmmm," said Layla. "Seems to me you're awfully proud of the fact that you were humble. Isn't that counter-productive?"

"Counter-productive?"

Layla rolled her eyes, and folded the list of faults. "Really, Zainab. Everyone knows what counter-productive is."

"I don't. Can't you tell me? I'd really like to learn a new word," I said humbly.

"Look it up in the dictionary."

"But you already know what it means. Why can't you just tell me?"

"Humph. I see you're still as lazy as ever. We had crossed that off, but I'm going to have to add it again." She unfolded the list. I looked over her shoulder. After the entry "kinship — doesn't respect bonds of kinship;" and "knowledge — doesn't bother trying to gain more knowledge," she wrote "lazy — can't be bothered finding things for herself." It was before "mischief-maker — likes to cause trouble."

I bit back a retort. I didn't want to be accused of rudeness. I could just see it, "rude — talks back to her elders." I climbed into bed, thanking Layla for her concern, and turned out the light. It had been such a productive day, and here again I felt like I had so far to go before I would be good enough.

It took a long time for me to fall asleep. It seemed Layla fell asleep immediately. I listened to her steady breathing long into the night.

12

In the morning though, I couldn't be down.

The wind had blown up during the night, from the south, melting the flimsy layer of snow, snatching the last few stubborn leaves that clung to the bare branches and hurling them skyward. If this kept up, it would be a muddy, green Christmas. I rounded the curve before the school, my hair flying out and around me. The trees lining the soccer field greeted me, waving in unison, cheering me on, bursts of sunshine peering through the murky cloud cover, lighting the path to Deanford. Life was good. Kevin wasn't so bad.

We had till the end of February. We could be ready by then. We still had time, if we hurried.

When the bell rang, and we'd settled down in class,

I asked Mr. Weiss if I could make an announcement. I stood at the front, my palms sweaty, my voice shaky. "Um, we'll be having the first rehearsals this afternoon after school. Anyone interested in playing a part or helping backstage, come to the gymnasium."

Cheryl glanced at Kevin and smiled gratitude. Jenny saw the exchange and hunched deeper in her seat.

Mr. Weiss got up, smiling. "Anything else?"

I shook my head and sat down.

For the rest of the day, nothing went wrong. Everyone treated me kindly, attentively. It felt strange.

When school finished, within minutes the gymnasium was full. I was so busy assigning people to be in the crowd, or other non-speaking roles, and do backstage duties that I didn't have time to worry where Kevin was. Or Jenny. I'd at least expected her to show up. She was my assistant.

Half an hour late, they strolled in. The whole gang of them. Emperor, Queen, Chamberlain, Tailor 1 and Tailor 2. And at the end, Jenny.

"Well," said Kevin, "you can give us our scripts."

I fumbled through the stack of them for his copy.

He looked around the busy gym, his nose wrinkled. "What a mess. You won't get any actual rehearsing done today, will you?"

I shook my head, picking up the stack of scripts. "Kevin, I didn't get a chance to highlight all your lines. You can take a marker, or pencil crayon, anything, it doesn't matter, and either underline or highlight every time you speak."

Kevin's face contorted in rage. "What! You expect

me to go through this whole script? What kind of show do you think you're running? Have you forgotten that I'm the one doing you a favor?"

Jenny stepped forward. "Um, I'll do it. You know, if you don't mind."

I smiled at her. "Would you? Thanks so much."

But Kevin grabbed her wrist. "Oh no you won't. I'm going to need you. Zainy, you'll just have to take care of it yourself."

Cheryl put her hand on her hip. "What about mine?"

I still had the stack of scripts in my hands. Before I knew what was happening, Kevin patted me on the head. "Be a doll and do Cheryl's too. And while you're at it, maybe you could do these guys' as well."

I said, "No way. They can do their own."

Kevin cocked an eyebrow. "Do you forget that I'm a professional actor? I'm used to being dealt with in a professional way. The director always highlights the actors' parts. If you're not going to be professional about it, you can just forget it. I mean really!"

I bit my tongue and fumed in silence.

Kevin turned toward the gym doors. "Let us know when you'll have the real rehearsal."

They were leaving. I called out, "Tomorrow. We'll start the real rehearsals tomorrow. Right after school. Be on time. Please."

Kevin was laughing at something Cheryl had said. Jenny gave me an apologetic look, and followed them.

There was nothing left to do but let all the other kids go too. I didn't feel like lugging five scripts home, so I picked up a marker and sat down cross-legged on the floor.

The squeak of the felt-tip markers was the only sound beside the hum of the fluorescent lights.

By the time I was finished, and had put away all the scripts for tomorrow, it was getting dark. The warm wind from this morning had turned bitter cold. It buffeted me all the way home, messing my hair, driving it into my face so I couldn't see.

When I finally trudged through the door, I hadn't even taken off my jacket when Layla came up to me. "You're late. You missed Zuhr and Asr and it's already time for Maghrib. You'd better get going and pray."

I nodded, humbly. "Thank you for reminding me. I'll do it right away."

She smiled, satisfied.

After I'd prayed, I didn't crash on the sofa like I usually did. I went and asked my mother if she needed help with supper.

She looked surprised and pleased. "Sure, you can peel the potatoes."

I sat down at the kitchen table, my legs aching, and I realized how long it had been since I'd rested. I hoped my mother and I could have a talk, but Waleed and Seema were fighting, and she had to call Layla to come stir the pot while she went to pry them apart.

Layla said, "How come you're so late?"

I didn't want to tell her so I just shrugged and said nothing.

"How come you're so late?"

I mumbled, "I had work to do."

"What kind of work?"

"Just work."

My mother came in just then and took the wooden spoon from Layla. Layla turned to her. "Ami, you know Zainab was late."

"Yes, Layla, I know that."

Layla put her hands on her hips. "Aren't you going to ask her why?"

My mother frowned. "Don't you have homework?"

When Layla was gone, my mother said, "What kept you so late at school?"

"It's that play I'm working on."

"Oh. Well, try not to come home after dark. I worry about you."

"Okay." I finished peeling the last potato and handed her the bowl. If she'd asked me, I would have poured out the whole story, but she didn't, so I kept quiet.

I tried to get to bed early, but I couldn't sleep. I was still trying hard to relax when Layla stormed into the room, turned on the big overhead light and shook my shoulder to wake me up.

I didn't say a word through my list of faults that night. But I found it hard not to fight back. Maybe I was arrogant. Why did I find it so hard to admit I wasn't perfect?

Finally, I heard Layla turning in her bed. "I think that's enough for tonight, Zainab. Shab-khair."

I returned her "Shab-khair." Which means good night, but I had a feeling I would not have a good night.

13

We didn't have a rehearsal the next day either. Kevin and his gang didn't show up. When I asked him about it the day after, during library, he shrugged. "I didn't know."

"But I told you. When you and your friends were leaving the gym."

He grinned. "I guess I didn't hear you."

"Well, we're having another rehearsal this afternoon, so please come on time."

"Yeah, sure." He turned and walked off laughing with his friends. Jenny didn't follow.

She had her hands in her jean pockets, and stared at her runners, scuffing the ugly brownish-yellow carpet. "How's the play going?"

I sighed and sank down into a chair. "It isn't. Christmas holidays start next week and we haven't even had one proper rehearsal. Can't you talk to Kevin? You know, remind him of his promise?"

Jenny bit her lip. "Um, I don't know, I mean, if I pressure him too much he might just forget about the whole thing."

"Yeah, I guess so. It's just that we've got to get going. Do you know if they've even started memorizing their lines? I gave them their scripts yesterday."

"Um, I'm not sure, they might have. Actually, yes. I think Cheryl has."

Great! Cheryl only had four lines.

Jenny touched my shoulder. "Um, I'm sorry I haven't been much of a help. I wanted to. It's just that . . . Kevin."

"It's okay, Jenny. You got him to agree."

Her bangs hid her eyes. She bit her lip, mumbling, "Yeah."

She looked like she wanted to say something, but just then Kevin called. Jenny jumped, flashed me an apologetic smile and ran to see what he wanted.

When school finished, I waited for them to show up. The kids who were going to be in the crowd were the same ones painting the sets and getting the costumes ready. Three kids, including Fran and Dan, the geometry twins, were making the costumes. The geometry twins were in charge of the hats. They were really just cardboard cones with flimsy scarves flowing out of their pointed ends, the kind that ladies used to wear in long-ago times. Fran kept measuring the sides to make certain they formed perfect isosceles triangles. And Dan kept remeasuring to be sure they were exact.

Five kids worked on the scenery, painting old-fashioned buildings with turrets, towers, battlements and flags, that we'd hang on the back wall of the stage to make it look like a town.

I glanced at the clock. Ten minutes late and there was still no sign of Kevin. Then Jenny walked in. Her hair covered a lot of her face, but not enough. I could see the blotchiness of her cheeks, and the tip of her nose was red and swollen. I met her halfway, hooking my arm through hers. "What's the matter, Jenny? What happened?"

She sniffed. "Nothing."

"Was it Kevin?"

Her lower lip was quivering. She hung her head, covering her face with her hands.

"What happened?!"

Jenny shook her head, her limp hair swishing back and forth.

I gave her a squeeze. "Jenny. What happened?"

She sobbed, "He told me to get lost."

"Why?"

"I asked him — I tried, Zainab, I really tried. He said I was nagging him. He told me to stop being such a . . .!" Her face twisted. "A bitch!" She broke down sobbing into my shoulder.

Everyone had stopped working and was staring at us. I led Jenny out of there, calling to them, over my shoulder, to keep working, I wouldn't be gone long. I took her to the washroom, turning on the cold water so she could wash her face and compose herself. She bent over the sink, cupping her hands, filling them with icy water and gulping it down. Her breasts sagged, brushing the rim of the sink. When she straightened, I handed her a paper towel and she blotted her face dry.

I tore another piece of paper towel and held it ready. "How dare he! That idiot!"

She stared down at the crumpled towel in her hand. The corner of her mouth twitched. "I was nagging him. He hates that. I should have known better."

"Don't blame yourself."

"But he told me to stop. If I'd listened . . ."

"He didn't need to call you that."

She was silent, twisting the damp paper round and round.

As I watched, her eyes filled with tears again. She chewed her lip and kept wringing that poor paper towel so tight that her knuckles were white. I swallowed, and said in a creaky voice, "I pushed you into this."

She avoided my eyes. "Don't feel guilty. I mean, I'm not doing it because of the play, well, not only because of it."

"But, Jenny . . ."

She took a deep breath and pulled out a compact, patting some makeup around her eyes and nose to cover the blotchiness. I never knew she wore makeup.

I tried again. "But, Jenny, look how he's hurting you. It's not worth it."

She shut the compact with a snap. "Um, I know you mean well, Zainab, but don't worry, really. I'll be okay."

I felt dismissed again, like in the classroom.

In silence, we returned to the gym. Neither of us mentioned Kevin during the next fifteen minutes. We just worked along with the others till 4:30, and it was time to go home.

I asked, "Are you going to walk home with me?"

She avoided my eyes. "I don't think so. I mean, I think I'll go by Kevin's house."

I wanted to shake her, tell her to have some pride, tell her she didn't need him. Instead, I nodded and said I'd see her tomorrow.

All the way home, the cheery Christmas lights depressed me.

I was cold, like an icicle, like a stupid, polyester-covered icicle, just hanging from an eavestrough, waiting for the icicle next to me to fall crashing to the sidewalk below. Doing nothing to save it.

An hour after I'd got home, and prayed and eaten a warm meal, I was still so cold I wondered if I'd ever be warm again.

I offered to wash the dishes, though it was Layla's turn. I turned the water to scalding and submerged my fingers for as long as I could stand it. The water was hot, but it didn't warm me.

How would I ever help Jenny? Had I done all I could? If I'd insisted . . .! If I canceled the play, would Kevin leave her alone? He hadn't before. Why would he now? And it seemed she didn't want him to. It wasn't my fault. But why did it still feel like it was? I doubled my pace and finished the dishes in record time. Layla was wiping the counters, watching me.

She followed me into the rec room and when I picked up the telephone receiver and was about to dial Jenny's number, she pressed down the button and disconnected the line. "Who are you calling?"

"A friend."

"A boyfriend?"

"No, just a friend."

"Who?"

I clenched my teeth so I wouldn't say something I'd regret.

Layla threw up her hands. "I give up! I talk to you and talk to you but it does no good. How on earth can I help you if you won't talk to me?"

I put down the receiver and told her about Jenny. I told her how Kevin was treating her and how it was all my fault. When I told her I was canceling the play she cried, "What! Are you stupid?! You're going to throw all that work out the window just because a girl is fooling around with a guy? You're nuts, Zainab, you really are!"

"But he called her a bitch. He doesn't care about her, he just wants one thing."

She wrinkled her nose. "And you think this Jenny is all innocent? What was she doing before you even started the play, fooling around in the classroom? Doesn't sound like any of that's your fault. These non-Muslim girls are like that. Didn't you know? They don't care about anything but boys. And talking to her won't make her stop. So you might as well just shut up and do your play."

Jenny wasn't like that. I shook my head. "I have to talk to her. I have to at least try."

Layla's jaw dropped open. She stared at me like I'd turned orange with blue polka dots. Then she moved away from the telephone and dusted her hands. "Fine. Don't say I didn't warn you."

With fingers that shook, I dialed Jenny's number. On the first ring, she answered. "Kevin?"

"Hi, Jenny. It's me, Zainab."

"Oh. Hi."

I cleared my throat. "I just called to say that I've decided to cancel the play. You don't have to sweet talk Kevin anymore."

"Um, really? But why?"

"I can't see you hurt like this. It's not worth it."

"You don't have to do that."

"I think I do."

"But, Zainab, I'm feeling better now, really I am. You don't have to worry."

I took a deep breath. "He may be the cutest guy in the whole school, but he's no good for you."

There was a pause. "He's not always mean. Sometimes, he's wonderful."

"You deserve better."

She laughed bitterly. "Yeah, sure."

"There must be someone out there who'll treat you nicely. You don't deserve this."

"I don't want anyone else."

"But, Jenny, really. You must know he's no good for you."

"I can't help it, Zainab. I love him."

I bit my lip. Silence dragged on. Finally I said, "Just don't do anything you might regret."

Her voice trembled. "It might be too late."

"What do you mean?"

There was a sob, and the sound of the receiver rubbing fabric. Then Jenny came back on. "Um, I'm really sorry, Zainab, I have to go. When you called, I thought it was . . . someone else."

"But, Jenny . . ."

"Bye."

Click. And then the dial tone. I was dismissed again. For that stupid Kevin.

I looked up and noticed that I still had the receiver in my hand and that Layla was watching me, her arms crossed over her chest. She said, "I told you so!" Then sauntered out of the room.

Gently, I hung up. At least I wasn't cold anymore.

I avoided Jenny for the next few days. It was easy. The only times I caught a glimpse of her were in class and whenever Kevin decided to show up for rehearsal.

At least the kids were starting to take the play more seriously. But only Cheryl knew her lines. Tailors 1 and 2 weren't too bad, and neither was the chamberlain. I got one of the geometry twins, Dan, to play the kid who has the guts to say the emperor is wearing no clothes. He was thrilled. He smiled so wide I thought his buck teeth would pop out.

Out of all of them, Kevin was the worst. He'd hardly read the script and he kept adlibbing, making up his own words. Like when Bill, the chamberlain, came in announcing the tailors, he was supposed to say, "Send them in. I will hear their petition!" Instead he said, "Okay. Let 'em in."

When we finished the last rehearsal before the holidays, I said, "Everyone please, for the sake of Mackenzie King, spend some of your holidays memorizing your lines, and practicing before a mirror. It'll make my job a whole lot easier. When we come back in January, we'll only have six weeks to polish it up. We'll need all the practice we can get."

They only half-listened. I heard papers rustling, feet shuffling, gum popping. They obviously wanted to get home. I finally dismissed them. I'd done the best I could.

Jenny was gathering up Kevin's books for him. I went up to her and cleared my throat. She looked up from kneeling on the floor, a text in her hand. I said, "Maybe we can get together during the holidays."

She glanced in Kevin's direction. "Maybe. I'll see how busy I am."

"Okay. Give me a call whenever you're free."

She shook some of the hair out of her eyes, grinning. "Sure."

"Jenny!" It was Kevin.

She started. "Sorry. Gotta go."

"Sure," I said. "Have a nice Christmas."

She looked back over her shoulder, smiling. "You too."

I sighed. Didn't she know I didn't celebrate Christmas? We do believe in Jesus (peace be upon Him), that he was a messenger sent by God. We just don't think Christmas has much to do with Him. (It's actually based on an ancient pagan festival celebrating winter solstice. Biblical scholars don't even think Jesus was born in December.)

I dawdled until the last kid had left and the caretaker had swept the gym, then I trudged home, wondering how I'd ever survive two solid weeks with Layla.

14

Within three days of staying home, I was bored. There was nothing to do.

We were sitting in the rec room watching T.V. when I felt thirsty and went to the fridge. There was only a little bit of juice left in the jug. It would be selfish of me to drink it. It would be unselfish of me to make some more. I checked the freezer. We were all out. So I put the jug back and got a glass of water, carrying it back into the rec room.

I had taken two sips when Layla cleared her throat, loudly. She was staring pointedly at me.

"What?" I asked.

She nodded at the glass in my hand, clearing her throat again.

I examined my water. Was there a bug in it or something?

Layla cleared her throat again, only louder.

"What is it?"

"I was hoping you'd realize for yourself, but I guess you're just as selfish as when we started your self-improvement plan."

"What do you mean?"

She sighed. "Do I have to explain it to you? Don't you realize? You really are hopeless, Zainab!"

"What did I do?!"

"Do you think you're the only one in this room that would like a glass of water?" She clucked her tongue. "How selfish can you get?"

"But if you wanted water why didn't you ask? I would have gotten it for you."

"I was testing you. I wanted to see if you would do it without being asked."

I couldn't believe it.

She continued, "For your information, the definition of selfish is someone who thinks only of their own needs. To be unselfish you must think of others' needs before your own. So if you weren't so selfish, it might have occurred to you that someone else might want some water too."

"But that's why I didn't take the juice. There was only a little left, and I thought someone else might want it."

"Well, that's a start. But to be truly unselfish means that you always think of other people's needs before your own, not just sometimes."

I couldn't argue with her about that. That would be truly unselfish.

She was staring at me. Chewing her lip, measuring me.

"What?"

"Never mind."

"What? Tell me."

"Well, if you must know, I'm just wondering whether this is working."

"What do you mean?"

"I'm just wasting my time. You'll never change."

"What do you mean?"

"It's your attitude. You'll never improve unless you want to. I'm not sure you want to."

"But I do. I'm trying, really."

She grimaced, shaking her head. "I'd like to believe you but I just get this feeling. Every time I tell you your faults, it's like you're resisting me. You don't want to hear them."

"But I do. I am changing. It just takes time."

Her head tilted to one side, her shoulders drooping, she looked at me as if I had been judged and the verdict was death by hanging. She got up to go. Tears welled up in my eyes. I begged her to stay, tell me how to change my attitude, help me any way she knew how. She said she might, later, she had to go call a friend. When she left she switched the T.V. off and the lights too.

I was cold. The room was dark as a grave. I shuddered, hugging my knees to my chest. I had to admit she was right. Maybe I did have an attitude. I did hate hearing my faults. Maybe I didn't want to change.

What if I didn't look at Layla's criticisms as attacks? What if, instead, I tried seeing them as suggestions? She was only trying to help me become a better person.

It was as if I was building a brick wall. Laying every brick carefully in place. Maybe I was too close to my wall. And if I was too close to it, I wouldn't be able to see if it was crooked or slanted or if one of the bricks was flawed. Layla was like a foreman, coming to point out the imperfections.

She was only trying to help me build a better wall. I smiled to myself. If I kept that image in mind it would be easier to accept the criticism in the spirit that it was intended.

I would try to seize every opportunity to prove to myself, and to her, that I was eager to change. I was eager for her criticism. I was going to build a fantastic wall.

In the morning, while I was fixing my bed, I glanced over at Layla's. It would be very considerate of me to make it for her — and very selfless — so I did.

I went in for breakfast, feeling happy about my good deed. Maybe this being selfless wasn't such a bad idea after all.

After breakfast, I jumped up, took the plate from my mother's hand and shooed her out of the room. I spent the next two hours cleaning the kitchen thoroughly. I whistled a happy tune while I was polishing the toaster.

When I was done, I called my mother in. Layla followed her. On the table was the newspaper and a cup of tea.

"Va! Va! Zainab." She picked up the toaster and grinned into the gleaming chrome. "I could use this as a mirror." Layla looked at it all, her lips pursed.

I smiled. "I'm glad you like it, Ami. What else can I do for you?"

She took a sip of her tea, sighing with contentment. (I'd even used freshly boiled milk for it.) "You've done enough for now. Why don't you go and play for a while?"

"Are you sure?"

"Oh yes."

"Okay, I think I'll go and read some hadith." As I passed Layla, I smiled up at her. I had her to thank for the change in me. She didn't smile back though.

I read for about an hour. I hadn't intended to read that long, it was just that once I started it was hard to stop. It was kind of fascinating to think that these were the actual sayings spoken by our Prophet, peace be on him, and here I was, one of his followers, reading them, understanding them, 1400 years later and thousands of miles away. It made me wish once again that I'd lived during his time.

One of the hadiths, a story the Prophet, peace be on him, told, really affected me. I couldn't get it out of my mind.

I closed the hadith book, a smile lingering on my face. Then the telephone rang, startling me. I picked it up on the first ring, hoping it was Jenny.

"Hi, Zainy?"

"Yeah."

"I got your number from the phone book."

"Oh." I still didn't know who was calling, but she sounded familiar.

"Don't know who it is, do you?"

A brownish-yellow face with a hooked nose sprang into my mind's eye. "Premini?"

"Yeah. How are you doing?"

"Okay."

"How's the play?"

I told her that the rehearsals were going a little better but that Kevin still didn't know all his lines.

I could hear the smirk in her voice. "I'm not surprised. Between all the girls he has, I don't see how he'd have time. Poor Jenny."

I bit my lip. Torn between wanting to know more and adding gossiping to my list of faults. "What happened?"

The smirk was back in Premini's voice. "It seems she caught Kevin with Cheryl. Can you imagine?!"

She'd dropped the receiver, I heard her laughing in the background. Poor Jenny for sure.

Premini came back on, gulping air, catching her breath. "Oh boy. Sorry about that. I dropped the phone."

"Where did you hear that?"

"Never mind. I just thought you'd like to know."

"How's Jenny?"

Premini sobered up. "I think she's all right."

"I hope so," I murmured.

Premini laughed. "Why should you care? She's not really your friend. Does she act like she gives a fig about you? It's all Kevin this and Kevin that. I told you she'd dump you as soon as she got in. It was just a matter of time."

"But she stood up for me. She's the only one who ever did."

Premini laughed bitterly. "Why're you looking to others to stick up for you? What's wrong with you sticking up for yourself?"

I couldn't answer.

She went on, "There's no difference between you and her. She's just a bit more obvious in chasing after Kevin."

"You finished?" I said coldly.

"Yeah, I'm done. I'll shut up now. Maybe you should call Jenny. Cheer her up."

"Okay, I will. Thanks for calling, Premini."

"Sure."

I didn't hang up, just pressed down the button to disconnect the line, and immediately dialed Jenny's number.

I waited and waited. I was about to hang up on the tenth ring when someone answered.

"Hi!"

"Jenny? Is that you?"

"Oh, hi, Zainab. I thought you were someone else. How are things going?"

I toyed with the telephone cord, winding it around and around my finger. "Boring. Why don't you come over?"

"Um, I'd really like to, but I should hang around in case Kevin calls. What about you? You might, you know, come over."

Then there was silence on her end of the line. Until Jenny hissed, "That's mine. Take it off."

I said, "Jenny? Are you talking to me?"

She didn't hear me. I think the receiver was away from her ear. I couldn't hear so well. She said, "Take it off, right now!"

"Is that how you talk to your mother?" came another voice.

"Take it off, please."

I heard Ms. Roberts say, "Don't be silly, you don't even like it."

"I do so. Grandpa gave it to me."

"What's wrong with you? Once I catch me a rich husband you can have ten shirts like it if you want."

Jenny said, "Take it off or I swear, I'll rip it off!"

I couldn't believe it. This was quiet, shy Jenny? I felt like I was in the coat closet again, all hot and uncomfortable. I shouldn't be listening, this was between Jenny and her mom.

Jenny dropped the phone and I heard snarling, screaming and then the unmistakable sound of tearing.

Ms. Roberts screamed, "Look what you've done! Stupid!! You've ruined it."

Jenny cried, "I don't care. Give it back."

"What's the point? It's ruined."

"Give it back, anyway."

"Fine!"

Suddenly there was a terrible jolt as the receiver fell on the floor. The sound of hasty footsteps, then someone picked up the receiver. "Zainab? Are you still there?"

"Jenny?"

Her voice shook. "Sorry about that."

"Are you okay?"

She sputtered, sobbing and gasping at the same time.

"Jenny?"

"I have to go. Bye."

I asked my mother if I could run over to Jenny's. She gave me a strange look but said okay. Within minutes I was out the door.

I stood for a moment at the end of Jenny's street, pushing my hair behind my ears every time the wind hurled it into my face. Garbage cans rolled noisily past me. Old dead leaves and twigs skittered across the road, trying to escape. The lawns were mounds of soggy turf, oozing mud at their edges. And the wisps of smoke that rose from the chimneys and vents were glad to ride free on the wind.

I shouldn't have been so eager to come. I walked down toward the last house before the railway tracks, her house, like an actor who didn't know his lines.

I stood in front of that gaping hole in her screen, not ringing the bell. What on earth would I say? I stared at the twisted wire that framed the hole, my feet turning to ice.

I felt the faintest of vibrations, like someone had come out into a hallway of the house. What if it was her mother? In panic, I looked around for someplace to hide. There was no time. The vibrations came louder, and with a squeak, the doorknob turned.

Quickly, I rang the doorbell. Jenny answered the door, wearing her jacket.

"Zainab!"

"I was worried. The way your phone call ended."

There was a twitch in the corner of her mouth. "Everything's fine . . . really."

She had her gloves tucked under her arm. She began putting them on, one finger at a time. "Um, I was just going out."

She wore lipstick. Blood red. It was too bright for her pale skin. And there were two smudges of blush on her cheeks like someone had slapped her, twice!

She finished putting on her gloves and glanced at me. "Did you want something?"

"Are you okay? How are things with Kevin?"

Her face turned red, till the blush almost blended in. "Um, actually, that's where I'm going now. Everything's fine, really."

"I thought we could do something together. You know, go skating or sledding."

She chewed her lip, beginning to walk down the driveway. Automatically, I followed. "I'd really like that. It's just that, Kevin, well, he kind of doesn't want me to, you know, talk to you too much." She laughed nervously. "He thinks you're, well, never mind."

We'd come to the bus stop. Jenny had her head bent, searching through her tiny little purse for a bus ticket. She continued, "And really, um, you know, the holidays are almost half over. I just don't see that we'll have time."

The bus pulled up in front of her and the door slid open. Jenny gave me a quick hug, and I got a whiff of her perfume. It was strong. "Anyway, it was nice of you to check on me." She hopped up the bus steps and dropped her ticket in, then she ran to the window, shoved it open and yelled out as the bus pulled away, "By the way, he is learning his lines. I'm making him."

I trudged home, feeling stupid. Wondering why I bothered about Jenny.

15

That night, in my room, I tried to smile, to show Layla that I was eager for her criticism. But I felt like I'd swallowed a rock, a big, black, smooth rock, and it was sitting in the pit of my stomach.

She read from her list. "You're arrogant, you think you're better than everyone else, you're nosy, you talk vain conversation —"

I cleared my throat. "Pardon me, Layla. I really don't mean to argue with you. I'd just like to know when I talked vain conversation?"

She frowned, staring at the ceiling for a moment. "This afternoon, when you were talking with that friend. Oh! And you've been back-biting."

"When was I back-biting?"

She narrowed her eyes. "You know very well. When your friend called, you were talking about that girl with the big breasts."

I sat up, clenching the blankets so tightly my knuckles hurt. "How do you know what I was talking about?"

"I just picked up the phone to call my friend. I couldn't help overhearing a little."

"But you should have hung up. You shouldn't have listened."

"Why? Do you have something to hide?"

I bit my lip and held silent.

"You still don't tell me anything. You're still too arrogant to let me help you. You think you know it all."

"I'm afraid that's not true, Layla. I told you about the play, I told you the problems I was having."

She thought for a minute. "Okay. You did tell me about that. And you have been a bit more considerate and less selfish."

With that little bit of praise, though it was given grudgingly, the stone in the pit of my stomach melted a little, though it didn't go away.

"Wait a minute. You told me about the play but you didn't listen to me. You didn't do what I told you to do."

"But aren't I allowed to do that? I mean, I listened to your advice but isn't it up to me to take it or not?"

"It just proves that you think you know it all."

"But I don't think that."

"You're arguing with me. See? You can't take criticism."

I clenched my jaw and waited for her to finish.

She covered her face in the white paste then started

patting on the baby powder, the innocent baby smell of it invading my side of the room.

She was quiet for a while. Was she finished? I peeked at her, she jumped into bed, pulled up the covers and reached over to shut off the lamp.

I said, "Anything else?"

"Yeah. Girls aren't supposed to whistle."

"Thanks, Layla. I really appreciate it."

"No problem. Shab-khair."

"Shab-khair." I rolled over, away from her. I closed my eyes and saw my brick wall. Slowly I took off some bricks; they were an earthy red. I took off two rows. With all my might, I hurled them into blackness. The wall was built on behavior. Tomorrow, I would adjust my behavior and tomorrow night when I examined my wall, it should be better.

By the time Layla gave me my list of faults the next night, I had replaced the two rows I'd removed. But according to her, I was still all the things she'd complained about the night before, plus now I was a show-off and sneaky. I ended up taking away three rows of bricks.

The last day of the holidays, I was sitting in the rec room, in the dark, in the silence, doing nothing. I felt like those three monkeys, see no evil, hear no evil, and do no evil. The problem was that even when I did no evil, Layla still criticized me for doing no good either.

My mother came in, turning on the light. She jumped. "Zainab! You gave me such a fright. Why are you sitting there in the dark? Why don't you go do something?"

"Like what?"

"Go and play."

"I don't want to play."

"Read some hadith."

"I already read six pages."

"Why don't you call your friend?"

I thought about Jenny, my eyes tingling. I didn't have any friends.

She continued, "Go skating. Do something! But don't just sit there."

I said, "Is there any work to do? I could clean the washroom."

She frowned at me. "You cleaned it yesterday. Go out and play. Get some fresh air. I worry about you."

"Okay, Ami."

I didn't want to go skating with Layla, and I didn't want to go alone, so I hauled out the telephone book, and looked under "G". I figured her phone number wouldn't be hard to find, there couldn't be more than one Gupta family in Glen Hollow. Moments later, Premini's phone was ringing.

She sounded happy to hear from me. We agreed to meet at the school's ice rink.

Premini was a lousy skater. At last, something I could do better than her. I picked her up off the ice many times.

"How do you do it, Zainab?"

I skated backwards, circling her. Then stopped. I was showing off. Humbly I said, "It's easy. Really. Take my hand."

She took a step forward. I wanted to laugh, but I

didn't. Her feet still thought she was walking. I held her arm and she managed a wobbly glide. "That's it," I said. "You can do it."

I let go. She grabbed for my arm, and lost her balance, falling flat on her behind with a thud that must have hurt. I pulled her up. "Are you okay?"

She nodded, gritting her teeth. "Just get me over to the side." She sat with the heels of her skates scraping the surface of the ice. "Don't let me stop you."

I sat down beside her. "It's okay." The ice was kind of bumpy, there were a few cracks, but no nicks or dangerous parts. I wanted to skate some more. I looked over at her. She was watching me.

"Go ahead, Zainab. Skate. I'll just sit here and watch you."

"Sure you don't mind?"

She gave me a shove. "Go on."

For a while there was only the scraping sound of my blades on ice. I felt free, like I'd grown wings on my feet, gliding just above the surface of the rink. I was fast — fields and trees and houses a blur — and yet in full control.

I slowed down and did a few lazy figure eights. Premini said, "Did you talk to Jenny?"

The teeth on the toe of my skates caught in the ice and I almost tripped. For a moment, I'd actually forgotten all about Jenny. While I skated backwards in a circle, crossing over and changing feet, I told Premini about my encounter with Jenny a few days before.

Premini continued, "Has Jenny actually started wearing makeup?"

"Yeah."

She had a wicked gleam in her eye. "I bet she and Kevin are . . . you know."

I skidded to a halt. "Shut up! You just shut up!"

"Okay. Okay. Sorry. Didn't mean to get you mad."

I didn't feel like skating anymore. I went to the side of the rink, plunked down and began untying my laces.

Premini put a hand on my arm. I pulled my arm away. "What are you doing, Zainab?"

"Going home. I've had enough."

"I'm sorry. I didn't mean anything."

Staring at the cracks in the ice, I made myself calm down. She was trying. I should try too.

Premini was quiet, fiddling with the laces of her skates.

I said, "She isn't like that. She's a good kid."

She smiled apologetically. "If you say so."

"I guess I'd better be going anyway."

Premini nodded, pulling at her laces. "Yeah, me too. I've got some work to do."

We took off our skates and put on our boots in silence. Tying the laces together, I slung my skates over my shoulder.

We stood up at the same time, avoiding each other's eyes, neither of us wanting to leave. Premini said, "So how did you spend the holidays?"

"Reading hadiths."

"What are they?"

"Things the Prophet, peace be on him, said. You want to hear one?"

"Not really."

We walked along the road and I told her a story from one of the hadiths anyway, about a guy who'd killed some people and wanted to be forgiven. She listened. When I was finished she said, "That's a strange story. It doesn't have a happy ending."

"Lots of stories don't have happy endings."

"Name some."

I shrugged. *Romeo and Juliet, Gone with the Wind, Casablanca.*"

"And he killed so many people. Did he really think he should be forgiven?"

"I think so. He was really sorry. Besides, if there was no hope for forgiveness, why would anybody stop doing bad things? The whole point of the hadith is that it's never too late to change."

"What about all those people he killed?"

"In another hadith it says that anybody who is murdered is like a martyr and will go to heaven."

"I don't know. It's kind of strange."

"You mean you don't like it?" I thought of her remark about eating meat and eggs.

"Well, it doesn't make much sense."

I stopped walking, my hands on my hips. "It makes more sense than bowing to a statue with an elephant head on it."

She pursed her lips and said, "We don't worship the statue. The statue is just a representation of one of God's attributes. Actually we believe in one God. We just believe He shows Himself in different ways."

I shook my head. "Still sounds like idol worship to me."

Premini opened her mouth to argue, I raised my hand to stop her. "I don't want to hear about it. I only said that because you said ours doesn't make any sense and you made fun of me because I eat meat."

We came to Charles Street. Premini had to turn down it to get home. We stood for a while on the corner, staring at our slushy boots. Finally Premini said, "Maybe we shouldn't talk about religion if we want to be friends."

I nodded. "Okay. I won't bug you about the stuff you do and you don't bug me about the things I eat."

She grinned. "It's a deal."

We tore off our mittens and shook hands. She crossed the street, walking down Charles Street, waving over her shoulder. "See you tomorrow, Zainab. A new year of school."

I started walking too and waved back. "Yeah."

A new year. I wondered how much Kevin had practiced. And I wondered how Jenny was.

16

I knew I shouldn't bother. But I felt like calling on Jenny bright and early the next day, the first day back. So I did.

She answered my knock wearing a tight sweater, cut low over her huge breasts and tucked into her tight Lucky jeans. Her hair was drawn back into a limp ponytail. Her eyes were lined in pitch black and her lips were blood red. There was a layer of makeup plastered on her face. It didn't hide the pimples, just coated them so that they looked like tiny volcanoes covered in beige snow.

"Are you ready?" I asked, trying not to stare at her face.

She pulled on her jacket and closed the door

behind her. She said, "Um . . . how was your holiday?"

"Boring. But yesterday I went skating with Premini."

"Really? How was it?"

"Okay."

"Do you think, you know, that you're becoming friends?"

"I guess so."

She grinned. "I knew it. I just knew you'd get along."

"What about your holidays?"

She chewed her lip. "Well, they certainly weren't dull."

"Anything interesting happen?"

Beneath the beige powder, she reddened. She bent her head, as if expecting her hair to fall into her face. Then checked herself. "Umm. I'd really, you know, rather not talk about it."

I shrugged, as if I didn't care.

When we neared Deanford, Jenny glanced around at the other kids who were sharing the sidewalk. "Um, Zainab. Can I ask you a favor? Please? I hope you understand."

"What?"

"Can we just, you know, separate a bit before we get to school? Kevin won't like it if we've been, you know, walking together."

I stopped in my tracks, letting her continue. She paused a few paces ahead, watching me over her shoulder. I should be angry. I had every right to be. But instead, I ached. Deep in the pit of my stomach, the smooth black rock was back, like I was its home. Other kids passed us, staring. I felt them brush by. I stood firm, frozen to the sidewalk. She was still watching me. I could sense her concern but I ignored her. I wasn't going to smile and say it was okay. Not this time.

"Zainab . . ."

I stared at the cracks in the sidewalk.

"Zainab? Please . . ."

"Just go, Jenny."

"I'm sorry, but if Kevin . . ."

"It's okay, really." There. I'd said it after all.

For a few more moments, she stood watching me, undecided. I dared to hope she would stay.

Then she said, "Please, understand." She turned and continued walking to school.

I was as cold as an icicle. I wanted to stand there forever till I turned into a statue. But after a long time, my feet got restless. My polyester pants made my leg itch, where the thread scratched my skin. I sighed and gave it up. Besides, I'd get in trouble for missing school.

I walked slowly. It was easy. I wasn't eager to get to school anymore. But even then, Jenny was barely a dozen paces ahead of me. And she kept glancing back over her shoulder.

Kevin and his gang were exchanging hockey cards. Laughing loudly, slapping each other on the back and looking at the pictures. Jenny walked toward Kevin. One of the guys tapped him on the shoulder. He looked up, saw Jenny and jammed the cards into his pocket.

He put his arm around Jenny's waist, possessively. She huddled into the crook of his shoulder. I huddled into the cold corner of the brick wall. I couldn't see Premini anywhere.

When the bell rang, Premini ran up and walked with me into the warm school.

I tried to ignore Jenny, but it was hard. My stomach still ached. And every time I started concentrating on math or history, or whatever we were studying, I'd hear Kevin whisper something or Jenny giggling at what he'd said. Then Mr. Weiss, or whoever was teaching the class, would say, "That's enough" or, "Jenny, quiet down," and the ache would return.

At recess all the guys and even some of the girls, like Cheryl, were passing around those hockey cards Kevin had been looking at. Laughing and gaping at them. Hiding them whenever the teacher or other kids came around. I'd never seen them so worked up.

When recess was over, I announced that there'd be a rehearsal after school. I didn't know what to expect.

The rehearsal started out ordinarily enough. Kevin came out on stage, wearing an imperial expression, striking a regal pose, one hand on his hip, the other gesturing to the chamberlain in a bored, kingly way to hurry up with the morning business.

The chamberlain read from his list, and then said, "By the way, sire, there are two tailors here to see you."

Kevin cocked his head, a puzzled look on his face. "Tailors?"

The chamberlain sketched a quick bow. "Aye, Your Majesty. They say they can weave you the finest suit of clothes you've ever imagined."

Kevin placed his forefinger on his chin, and strutted

across the stage. "How curious. Send them in."

They went through the whole play. Every word Kevin said was magical. Every gesture was perfect. I forgot I was sitting on a creaky wooden chair in a noisy auditorium as I watched the story unfold. The only time I had to direct was when the other actors, like the queen, that stupid Cheryl, and the chamberlain, messed up — I had to call to them to repeat their lines, and change their tone or attitude.

Even the kids working on the sets and costumes stopped for a moment to hear Kevin deliver his lines — and he did deliver them, he didn't just say them.

When Dan, the geometry twin, made his declaration that the emperor was wearing no clothes, Kevin actually blushed beet red. He continued to hold his head high as he finished the parade, but he portrayed the perfect amount of embarrassment and outrage. He made the audience know, just by the look on his face, that as soon as he got hold of those tailors he'd get even.

The curtain closed and there was silent awe.

I stood up, clapping. "Wonderful, Kevin. That was excellent. Repeat that performance at the competition and we're sure to win."

Kevin gave me a wary look. "You think so?"

"You were wonderful! I'm impressed."

He looked at me out of the corner of his eyes. "I guess I was better than Premini Gupta . . ."

I was taken aback. What should I say? Premini was different. With her, you could see the pain of Shylock. The feelings she portrayed were really there. It was obvious she'd felt them before. But Kevin just wore the feelings, he put them on like a costume. He was convincing enough, but not at all like Premini.

"Well?" he asked. "Was I?"

I smiled. "Yes, Kevin."

He looked pleased with himself. "You're okay, Zainy. Maybe we'll break the curse of Mackezie King."

"Maybe? There's no way we can lose."

I heard the gym door open. Jenny shuffled in. The chamberlain snickered at her. So did all the other guys working on the sets and scenery. Some of the girls were laughing too, glancing at Jenny, and covering their mouths to stifle the giggles.

What was going on? I yelled at them all to stop it, settle down and keep working. Was it because her hair was a mess? She'd taken out the ponytail and it was all back in her face. The lipstick was gone from her lips; they were their usual pale pink again now. With her lower lip trapped between her teeth, she came up beside Kevin and tapped him on the arm, whispering, "Um, Kevin, please, could I talk to you?"

Kevin's face was red and he didn't look at her. "Not right now, Jenny. I'm busy."

She tugged on his sleeve, her voice thick with tears. "Please, Kevin."

He yanked his arm away. "Not right now!"

On tiptoes, she leaned against him, and cupped her hand to his ear. I caught the words "pictures" and "you promised."

Kevin rolled his eyes and followed her to a corner of the room. They weren't quite whispering anymore, but with the hum of the fluorescent lights and the rustling of restless feet and the murmurs, we couldn't really hear them. Most of the workers were quiet, glue and scissors held in unmoving hands, their eyes fixed on Jenny and Kevin.

Jenny was crying, gesturing wildly with her arms. I'd never seen her so upset. Kevin listened with growing impatience. He kept glancing back at us, his face red and angry.

Cheryl smirked. She held a secret. Her friend leaned over and whispered in her ear. She giggled and whispered back. Then she took out some of the hockey cards I'd been seeing all around the school. What was it about those cards anyway? Why would girls be interested in them?

I picked up a piece of cardboard, pretending to be taking it over to the kids making the scenery and crept up behind Cheryl and her friend. Now I saw that they weren't looking at hockey cards at all. They were look- ing at photographs of something.

Some of the kids were on their feet. Others were rising. Jenny was screaming now, clawing at Kevin's chest. "You promised. How could you? I trusted you!"

Kevin glanced at his friends, laughing. He turned to go. She reached out and grasped his arm.

He turned slowly, staring at her hand on his arm. Time stood still. I wanted to run to her, but I was frozen to the spot. As if in slow motion, Kevin covered Jenny's face with the palm of his hand and shoved once, hard. Jenny fell back a step and collapsed onto the gym floor.

Pointing his finger at her crumpled form, he said,

"Don't you ever grab me again. Do you understand?"

Her body was wracked in sobs, heaving silently. The sight of her like that was more terrible than tears.

Calmly, Kevin tucked in his shirt where it had come free of his Lucky jeans, and taking out his comb, he tidied his already tidy hair. No one spoke. It was as if we'd all turned to stone, or were an audience, watching the scene on stage, unable to participate.

Then Premini and Mr. Weiss burst into the gym. "What's going on here?" Mr. Weiss bellowed.

Kevin looked surprised. "Ask Jenny. I'm leaving."

Mr. Weiss said, "No! You stay! Everyone else leave."

Cheryl, Bill, Tailors 1 and 2, the geometry twins, and everyone else filed out the door. As I was following, Mr. Weiss stopped me.

Then he turned to Jenny, pulling up his drooping pants and tucking in the tails of his shirt. "Jenny? Are you okay?"

I went and knelt beside her, trying to help her up. She was too weak, or else she refused. Premini joined me and, each taking hold of one of her arms, we hauled her up. She was still sobbing, and as limp as a soggy tea bag. We propped her against us.

Kevin leaned against the door-frame, his arms crossed, looking annoyed. Had he no feelings? Didn't he care at all?

Mr. Weiss looked into as much of Jenny's eyes as he could see through her hair. "Jenny? Did Kevin hit you?"

She was still crying but she managed to shake her head.

Kevin said, "See? Can I go now?" Without waiting for an answer, he picked up his jacket.

"Wait a minute!" Mr. Weiss bellowed. He turned back and said very gently, "Jenny, it's okay. No one will harm you. Just tell me what happened. Didn't Kevin hurt you?"

Vaguely, she nodded. "Um, yes. Um, no. I mean no. I did grab him first . . . ."

Mr. Weiss frowned, his bushy eyebrows joining in the middle. "Why did you grab him?"

She covered her face in her hands and shook her head, sobbing.

Premini said, "Was it because of the pictures?"

Kevin shouted, "Shut up, Gupta! Mind your own business."

Mr. Weiss said, "What kind of pictures were they?"

At the word "pictures," Jenny wailed, "No, no pictures. Never mind the pictures." She thrashed her head back and forth. Premini and I had a hard time holding her.

Mr. Weiss turned to Kevin. "What do you know about these pictures?"

Kevin blanched, dropping his arms to his side and standing straight. "Me? Nothing. I don't know anything about any pictures."

I cried, "He's lying."

Kevin roared, "Shut up! You can't prove a thing."

Mr. Weiss's mouth was a grim line. He said nothing.

Jenny stopped thrashing and hung her head, her hair hanging down in damp strands that clung together.

Mr. Weiss parted the curtain of hair, peering at Jenny's red swollen eyes and blotchy forehead. "Jenny? If Kevin hurt you, you can do something about it. Tell me and I can take appropriate action."

Jenny shook her head. "No."

Mr. Weiss frowned, "What did you say?"

"Um, he didn't hurt me. Um, I don't want you to do anything to him."

Kevin looked smug. "See? Now can I go?"

I cried, "No! I saw him push her down."

Kevin said, "It was self-defense! She hit me first."

I said, "She didn't hit you. She grabbed you."

Kevin looked triumphantly at Mr. Weiss. "It's still assault, right?"

Mr. Weiss avoided Kevin's eyes. "Well, kind of."

Kevin grinned. "See? There's nothing you can do. I didn't do anything." He sauntered out of the room without a backward glance. Mr. Weiss just let him go.

Through the veil of hair, Jenny watched. When he was gone, she buried her face in her hands and started sobbing again.

Mr. Weiss sighed. "Very well, maybe we should talk about it tomorrow. It'll give you a chance to calm down. Will you be okay? Do you want to talk about it tomorrow?"

She quieted, her hair completely covering her face, and nodded slightly.

He took her arm, and gently led her away from us. "I'll drop her off home. Maybe I can talk to her mother."

Jenny cried out, "No!"

Mr. Weiss patted her arm, soothing her. "There, there, everything will be okay." At the door of the gymnasium, he turned back to us. "Do you girls want a ride too?"

We both nodded.

Mr. Weiss tried asking Premini about the pictures but Jenny cried out, screaming at her, so she held silent. The rest of the way home, nobody said a word. I thanked Mr. Weiss for the ride. He just nodded, a grim look on his face, and drove off with Jenny.

17

As soon as I got home, I went in and prayed. After I'd finished, I made an extra little prayer for Jenny, asking God to let her be okay. I was still sitting with my scarf on, wondering about those pictures, when I heard a loud crash, and Seema screaming.

A few moments later, I heard Layla screaming too. I went to see what all the commotion was about.

Layla and Waleed were locked in a death-grip. He had one of his matchbox cars clenched in his fist, his eyes screwed tight, holding on with every ounce of strength, while Layla tried to pry his little fingers apart. Seema was watching.

I asked Seema, "What happened?"

Seema pouted, "Waleed won't give me his car."

"But you have your own cars, why do you want his?"

Seema thought for a moment, retrieved a few of her own cars, and tapped on Layla's shoulder. "It's okay now. I'll just play with these."

By this time, Layla had pried away the car. She handed it to Seema. "Don't be silly. You said you wanted it, and here it is."

Waleed was sobbing. I couldn't bear to hear him. My mother wasn't home. She wouldn't be home for another half hour.

I wasn't going to say anything but when Waleed came to me for comfort, sobbing his heart out till my shoulder was damp with his tears, I couldn't stay quiet. Softly, I said, "It's not fair."

Layla turned and stared at me. "What did you say?"

I looked her right in the eye. "I said, it's not fair. Waleed just has a few cars that he's very attached to. Why'd you have to take them?"

Seema stared at me.

Layla sniffed, tossing her long black hair away from her face. "The Prophet, peace be on him, said part of someone's being a good Muslim is his leaving alone that which does not concern him." Then she turned on me, wrinkling her nose. "In other words, mind your own business."

I wasn't going to let her get away with it. Not this time. With all the hadiths I'd been reading, this time I was ready for her. I quoted right back, "The Prophet, peace be on him, also said, 'Whoever sees an injustice, let him change it with his hand; and if he cannot, then with his tongue, and if he cannot, then in his heart, and that is the weakest of faith.'" I had my hands on my hips, and I couldn't resist adding, "In other words, you're doing Waleed an injustice."

Layla's red face was inches away from mine. Her mouth was set in a grim line. Waleed had stopped crying and was watching us. Seema was watching us. I held my breath. I had her. She couldn't wriggle out of this one.

Then Layla said, "As my younger sister, you should not be criticizing me. Islam teaches that you must respect your elders. So you have no right to criticize me."

"Funny you should mention that, Layla, but do you know that in all the hadiths I've been reading, respect and obedience don't seem to go hand in hand?"

Layla's eyes were wide with astonishment. I guess I should have shut up, but this had been bugging me. "In fact, there were many companions of the Prophet, peace be upon him, who completely disagreed with their parents, and disobeyed them, even while they respected them."

"But those guys had parents who weren't Muslim. Your parents are Muslim. And so am I."

"I'm sure some of them were." I hesitated.

"Who? Who was?"

"Well, I'm not exactly sure of their names and stuff but I know it applies to Muslim parents too." I was going to tell her about a hadith that says there's no obedience to the creation of Allah, when it involves disobedience to the Creator. In other words, you don't

obey the people God made, when it means you're dis-
obeying God. But I'd lost my chance.

Layla went on, "You've got no proof. Find the
hadith and show it to me, and until you do, I don't
believe you. And besides, you would dare disobey
your parents, who care for you and gave you life? How
ungrateful can you get? I wonder what Ami and Abi
would think of that."

"No! Don't tell them."

"Why not? You're telling me this. Are you ashamed
to say the same things in front of your parents? What
kind of hypocrite are you?"

"I'm not a hypocrite!"

"Well, you're saying one thing in front of me and
another in front of them . . ."

"I'm just saying you should be fair."

There was a hint of anger in Layla's voice. "Don't
you believe in respecting your elders?"

There was only one answer to that. I couldn't argue
with the Quran. But hadn't I read that all Muslims
were supposed to be fair? Even the elders. I muttered,
"Yes, but . . ."

"Then do not criticize your elders."

Just then we heard the key in the lock, and the
shuffle of my mother's feet on the doorstep. Layla
fixed me with her venomous eyes, telling me clearly
that she wasn't done with me. It was so frustrating.
She was wrong. I just knew she was, but I couldn't
exactly prove it. When my mother called, "Assalaamu
alaikum," I ran out calling, "Ami, Layla's bullying
Waleed."

My mother stood on the doorstep, the rain dripping off her coat, making puddles on the floor, her arms weighted down with groceries.

Immediately, Layla took a shopping bag from my mother and said, "Ami, when you're gone from the house, who's in charge?"

My mother smiled at Layla and handed her the other bag. I should have helped her with the groceries.

My mother put down her purse and took off her coat. "Zainab. Have you been giving your sister a hard time?"

"But, Ami, she was being mean to Waleed."

"Zainab! You know very well that Layla is your older sister, and as your older sister, you must respect her."

Layla, standing behind my mother, stuck out her tongue at me. My mother continued, "After me, she is like a mother to you."

"But, Ami, she was wrong. She wasn't being fair. She was taking Waleed's own cars away from him just to give them to her darling Seema."

Seema and Layla glared at me. If looks could kill, I'd be dead.

My mother said, "Oh, what does it matter, a few cars? Waleed will get over it. I'm tired from shopping. I don't want to hear anymore."

Layla wore such a smug look on her face. It was too much. Suddenly it was just too much.

"It's not fair, Ami," I said. I was already in for it from Layla, I might as well make it worthwhile.

"What do you mean, bethi?"

"Every night Layla gives me a list of my faults, but I'm never allowed to tell her when she's doing wrong."

My mother frowned. "A list of faults? How long has this been going on?"

I perked up. And now Layla frowned.

My mother fixed her with a look. "Well?"

Layla smiled. "I was only trying to help. I was the one who told her we should stop. She really wasn't getting anything from them, but she insisted we continue. All she had to say was she didn't want them anymore. It's nothing to me if she doesn't want to improve herself."

"It's not that I don't want to improve myself," I said.

My mother had her eyes fixed on me now. "What is it then?"

Layla was looking at me, even more smugly than before. My mother was looking at me. And so were the twins, with their big round eyes. How could I explain? The way they made it sound . . . Oh, I should have left well enough alone.

Layla said, oh so softly, her voice dripping honey, "If the self-improvement sessions bother you, Zainab, all you have to say is stop it, and I'll stop. It's really up to you. I never meant to hurt your feelings. But everyone can use improving. No one, except God, is perfect."

My mother got to her feet and patted me on the shoulder. "Every now and then, we must all take a little teasing from our elders. That doesn't mean you don't respect them."

I avoided her eye, and Layla's triumphant expression.

My mother cleared her throat. "Is that understood, Zainab?"

"Yes, Ami."

My father had to work overtime, he's a carpet installer and there was a big job to finish, so Layla sat at the head of the table at supper. All through the meal, she kept sending me dirty looks. Tonight, my list of faults would be twice as long. I wondered if we'd be done before it was time for fajr prayer at dawn.

I could barely eat. I kept wondering about Jenny. What could have upset her so badly?

After supper, when Layla and I were cleaning the kitchen, the phone rang. I yelled, "I'll get it."

Layla threw down her dish towel. "No, you won't. I'll get it."

I continued washing the dishes, straining my ears to hear who was on the phone. It was a strange conversation from what I heard. Layla kept saying, "What! What! Speak louder. I can't understand you." Finally she hung up.

She came into the kitchen, a puzzled look on her face.

My mother looked up from her newspaper. "Who was it?"

"Some weirdo. I think she was drunk."

I almost dropped a soapy dish. She?

My mother said, "Oh dear! Was it an obscene phone call?"

Layla shrugged. "I'm not sure."

She'd just started wiping the table when the phone rang again.

I wiped my hands. "I'll get it."

Layla pushed me aside. "No, I'll get it."

This time, my mother and I could hear her yelling clearly from the kitchen. "Get lost. You creep!"

Layla stomped back into the kitchen. "The nerve! Same woman. Going 'Ze, ze, ze, ze' like she was some kind of bee or something."

I slipped out of the kitchen into the rec room and picked up the phone. Quietly, I dialed Jenny's number. It was busy. I hung up, a terrible feeling of foreboding in the pit of my stomach, and immediately the phone rang. I picked it up right away.

"Za, za, za, za, na . . ."

"Jenny? Is that you?"

A cry of relief on the other side of the phone, then, "Heh . . . heh . . ." She wasn't laughing. She wasn't panting. She was trying to say something.

"Help? Jenny, do you need help?"

There was another cry and then a clunk as the receiver must have fallen out of her hands.

I grabbed my jacket, and while I slipped on my shoes I called to my mother that I had to go over to Jenny's. An instant later, I was out the door and racing down the streets.

I slowed down as I neared her place. The house was dark, except for the back door area. The screen door with the hole in it swung open, creaking on its hinges. I tried to hurry but my feet were reluctant. Afraid of what?

The back door was half open, as if a burglar had entered. I tried to listen, over the pounding of my heart. I pushed the door open. Jenny lay on the floor of the entranceway, reaching out, her eyes closed.

What should I do? I'd read books where this kind of thing happened . . . I should check to see if she was alive. She was warm. A pulse throbbed in her throat. She was alive. I ran to the phone in the kitchen. My fingers shook. I dialed 911.

"Operator. Emergency. My friend's unconscious."

"What's the address?"

"Don't know. I came and she's lying in the hall." Tears splashed onto my wrist. I didn't have time for them.

"It's okay. I've got it. Help's on the way. Stay with her."

I hung up the phone, trembling. Back in the hallway, on the cold bare linoleum, Jenny looked uncomfortable. Should I move her? No. I read that you never move someone who's fallen. If their back's broken, it could paralyse them. Should I get a blanket? Yes. She might be in shock. Where? I don't want to go into the house. It doesn't feel right. Besides, what if a burglar's in there? I take off my jacket and put it over her. That's when I notice her wrists. They've been scratched with a blade, like she'd tried to slit them open, but couldn't do it. Jenny! Tried to kill herself. How could she? My eyes blur. What a time for tears. I can't cry now. I need to think. Jenny, what did you do? Why didn't you call me? Stupid!

Where's the ambulance? Why aren't they here yet? What's taking so long? Oh, Allah, help her.

Why was she unconscious? I search the entranceway

and her hair for blood. Did she fall and bump her head? No. No blood stains on the walls or her head. If she didn't slit her wrists, maybe she tried pills. That's it. That's why she'd sounded drunk. I should find them. Then I could tell the ambulance guys, what were they called? Para-somethings. Can't remember. Oh, it doesn't matter. Could tell them what she took. Would make it easier for them to treat her. I check the kitchen. Nothing there. Nothing but dirty dishes. In the bathroom, dirty grimy sink, flecks of blood and a brown prescription bottle that had rolled behind the toilet. It's empty. Some complicated drug name on the label. One white pill on the floor.

I grab it and shove it in the vial. Can't find the cap so I just hold my hand over top of it and run to see if Jenny's moved. She hasn't.

See some headlights shine on the screen door. Run to open it to the ambulance attendants. That's what they're called. No, silly me, paramedics, not attendants. Stupid! Doesn't matter! It wasn't the ambulance. It's Jenny's mother.

She sees Jenny. "What have you done to my baby?"

I try to tell her "Nothing," but she doesn't listen. Shoves me out of the way, kneeling beside Jenny, clutching her head to her breast, crying, mouth wide open, like a baby.

She screeches, "Do something! Call 911!"

"I did."

"Don't just stand there! Do something!"

"What?"

"Anything!"

I open the screen door and watch for the ambulance. Finally. Red and white flashing lights. A siren. They're here!

Jenny's mother shoves me out of the way again. Shrieking at the attendants, "Help my baby."

They ask questions. Calm. Efficient. She screams, "Hurry! Never mind about that!" They turn to me. I show them the vial. One smiles, nods and puts it in his pocket. They strap Jenny to a stretcher, careful not to move her back.

One of them wraps Jenny in a blanket. She looks white as snow. He turns and hands me my jacket. Jenny's mom pushes me out of the way again, climbs into the ambulance. They speed away in a flurry of lights and sirens. I'm alone. Forgotten. There's flecks of blood on the wrists of my jacket.

18

When I got home from Jenny's, Layla was waiting.

She shrieked, "Where do you think you went running off to like that?"

My mother frowned. "Layla, please. Let her at least take off her jacket and come sit down."

My mother's forehead was wrinkled with concern. "Come sit down, Zainab. Where did you go?"

"I told you. Jenny's house. I had to help her, there was no one home. She was lying unconscious when I got there. I called the ambulance."

"Haa Hai. Is she okay?"

I bit back the tears. "I don't know. Could I go to the hospital and see how she's doing?"

My mother shook her head. "I'm sorry, beta, but

that's not a good idea. Your father's got the car and besides, you'll probably just be in the way. It's better to visit her tomorrow."

When it was time for my self-improvement session that evening, I begged Layla to let me off for the night. But there was no way. She was plenty angry about my interference in the fight between Seema and Waleed. She gave me a long lecture. But I was only half listening. I kept wondering why Jenny would have tried to commit suicide.

What had Kevin done to her? Did he dump her? He must have. But what about those pictures?

The next morning, Premini came up to me as soon as I stepped onto school property. "Did you hear the news? Jenny tried to commit suicide! She slit her wrists. There was blood everywhere. The ambulance came and everything."

I didn't bother correcting her. "I know, Premini. Don't tell anybody."

She waved at the schoolyard. The kids were gathered around in groups; skipping ropes and balls lay abandoned. Everyone was talking in hushed tones. "They all know."

"Premini! How could you?"

"It wasn't me. Someone else told. I think Kevin's mom works at the hospital, in the emergency ward."

"But why? Why would Jenny do such a thing?"

Premini cocked her head to one side. "I think I know. Kevin and her had this huge fight."

"I know! I was there, remember?"

"Did you see the pictures?"

"What pictures? I heard her mention them when she was talking to Kevin, but I never saw any."

Premini's mouth hung open. "You never saw the pictures! You must be the only one in the whole school who didn't."

"What were they pictures of? Kevin and Jenny?" I laughed nervously.

"No. Worse. They were pictures of Jenny topless."

This time my mouth hung open. Jenny? Topless? "You mean no shirt or bra on?"

Premini nodded slowly.

"And everyone in the school's seen them?"

I grew hot just thinking about it.

I was silent, letting this news pile on top of all the shocking things that had happened since yesterday. No wonder Jenny was so upset in the gymnasium. No wonder she'd grabbed Kevin's arm. No wonder. No wonder.

I said, "Poor Jenny. How did she ever let him talk her into taking such pictures?"

Premini shrugged. "I guess some girls will do anything for 'luv.'"

Mr. Weiss came into view, shuffling along the blacktop, shoulders slumped, hands stuck in his pockets. His pants drooping dangerously low, and yet he didn't pull them up.

I walked up to him, Premini close behind me. "Mr. Weiss, did you hear what happened to Jenny?"

Beneath his bloodshot eyes, the baggy pouches were even baggier than usual. He said, "Yes, Zainab. Do you know anything about it?"

I glanced at Premini. There was no way I could nicely get rid of her. Besides, what harm could it do if she listened? The whole school already knew, pretty much, what had happened. I said, "Jenny called me last night. I was the one who found her and called the ambulance."

Mr. Weiss said, "Really? What happened to her mother?"

"I don't know. She got there after I did."

"She went out? I specifically told her that Jenny was in no state to be left alone."

I shrugged. "I found Jenny passed out by the back door. Her mother wasn't there."

The color drained from his face. Even his bushy moustache drooped with fatigue. He looked old. He wiped his hand down his face, sighing. I got the feeling that he blamed himself.

Premini said, "But is she all right? Will she live?"

Mr. Weiss nodded. "Oh yes. The ambulance arrived in time. I guess that's thanks to you, Zainab. But she's got a terribly sore throat — they had to pump her stomach. She'll be out of the hospital this morning."

I was so relieved tears came to my eyes. Thank Allah she'd be okay. When I got home that afternoon, I'd pray a few extra rakaats of nafil along with my Zuhr prayer.

The bell rang and I went into class with a lighter heart. Maybe I could buy Jenny a card and get all the class, including Kevin, to sign it. It would probably cheer her up. Or better than that, I could make one. She'd like that even more.

All during Math, I doodled on some blank paper, designing the card. I drew a little kitten — Jenny once told me she loved kittens — holding a note in its mouth that said *Hope you're feeling better*, and I put a bouquet of flowers at its feet. I was so excited I didn't hear the teacher call on me to answer a question. When I finally looked up, because everyone was staring at me, he just gave me a stern look, and warned me to pay attention or I'd have a detention.

By the end of Math class, I'd copied the kitten and flowers in good onto a clear sheet of paper and was beginning to color it in.

In English, Mr. Weiss was fidgety. He pulled his pants up, tucking his shirt in about three times before he realized it was already tucked in. Halfway through class, I finished coloring Jenny's picture.

Mr. Weiss was assigning grammar exercises when the intercom interrupted him. The secretary told him he had an urgent phone call. He glanced once at me, told everyone to behave themselves he'd be right back, and left the room.

As soon as the echo of Mr. Weiss's footsteps disappeared down the hall, Bill, who was playing the chamberlain in our play, stood up. He tried to keep his face straight.

There were giggles all over the class.

Kevin was sullen and quiet. Bill said, "Your emperor has learned that one of his subjects has tried to end it all."

Cheryl pinched the cloth of her blouse and pulled it out to form two big breasts. A laugh burst out of

Kevin. Then he scowled and told her to stop it.

I took a deep breath, trying to stop the tide of heat rising from my feet up to my throat. How dare he? How could he? He had absolutely no shame.

Bill and Cheryl both said, "Awe, poor Jenny."

There were more giggles across the classroom, but other kids were silent, watching.

Then Kevin held up one hand, while looking at his watch. "In honor of Jenny, we will hold a two minute silence. Sssshh! Starting . . . now."

For a few seconds, they just looked at each other. Cheryl at Kevin, Bill at Cheryl, Kevin at Tailor 1, Tailor 2 at Bill. And nobody said a word for Jenny. Nobody dared! The geometry twins just sat there twiddling their thumbs. Premini watched me, seeing what I would do. All the other kids just looked down, like a bunch of dummies. Kevin and his gang were breaking their own silence, giggling and snickering.

One of the boys said something about Jenny's breasts, and there was a fresh burst of laughter.

I felt sick. Nauseated by the cool, smug look on Kevin's face. How could they talk about Jenny like that? She'd never done a thing against anyone. How could they treat her like that? And the rest of the class just sitting quiet, not saying anything to stop them. Including me. Why? Because if I did, Kevin and all the others wouldn't be in the play.

Suddenly, I didn't care anymore. The only reason I'd taken on the play was for them to get to know me. They didn't want to know me. And now I knew them, I didn't like what I knew.

They couldn't accept Jenny, just because she had big breasts. Why would they ever accept me? I was really different.

I was just about to stand up and tell Kevin off, when Premini put her hand on my arm. "Zainab, sssh. Don't say anything."

I pulled my arm away. I had to say something. For Jenny. It took them a while to realize I was standing, silently glaring at Kevin.

I felt like my feet, through the soles of my shoes, would burn holes in the linoleum. My face was hot. My hair crackled with static. It buzzed around me like a force field. I couldn't see properly. Everyone was a blur of faces, muttering gibberish. Only Kevin stood out clear, distinct.

They stopped laughing. Kevin watched me.

I stared right into his wolf's eyes. My mouth was dry. My palms were hot and wet, but my voice came out steady. "How dare you, Kevin!"

Immediately the laughter left Kevin's face. All was quiet. Some blurred shapes, his friends, grouped around him.

I hissed, "You're nothing but a —"

"Shut up, Zainab," growled Kevin. "I'm warning you."

"I'm not scared of you," I lied. "How could you treat Jenny like that? You used her!"

"It's none of your business."

"You bastard!"

"Shut the hell up!"

"It's all your fault. You made her do it."

Kevin froze, his eyes the only part of him moving, shifting around, glancing at the others in the room. He was afraid!

I continued, "When the teachers find out, you'll pay for it. They'll . . ." I stalled. What was the punishment for something like this?

Kevin laughed. "They can't prove a thing. Anybody could have taken those pictures." He nudged Bill with his elbow. "Right, Bill?"

Bill came into focus, nodding slowly. A frown puckered his forehead. Tailors 1 and 2 were quiet, standing a few paces back. Only Cheryl still stood right next to Kevin now.

I clenched my fists so hard my nails bit into my palms. "How could you do that to Jenny?"

Kevin took a step forward. "Get this straight, Zainy! I didn't make her do anything she didn't want to do! If I ask her to do something and she does it, how am I to blame? It wasn't my fault. Besides, she's a nobody. A fool! You should have heard the things she said about you!"

"You liar! Damn you to hell!"

"Shut up, Zainab, or I'll —"

"You'll what? Leave the play? Go ahead. You're a lousy actor anyway." I put on the expression he'd worn in that movie where he was a newspaper boy, and said, "Which way did he go? That way, sir."

Some of the kids, quite a few of them actually, laughed. At Kevin! Kevin was as surprised as I was.

I said, "Premini's twice the actor that you'll ever be."

Someone said, "Yeah." I think it was Fran or Dan. I felt someone standing next to me. Was it Premini? I didn't dare take my eyes off Kevin to look. But it sure felt good not to be standing alone.

Bill and Cheryl shifted, ever so slightly, away from Kevin. He was on his own.

The person next to me spoke. It was indeed Premini. "You'd better sit down, Kevin. Mr. Weiss is coming."

Everyone took their seats. I didn't rush. Kevin dawdled, waiting till the last moment and trying to slip into his chair nonchalantly, as if he wasn't really scared of Mr. Weiss.

Mr. Weiss walked in and looked straight at me. My face felt flushed. I was still hot, and my heart hammered a fast beat. Then he looked at Kevin. Bill, Cheryl and the others whose desks were close to Kevin's had pulled them away a bit. Leaving the rows skewed, and Kevin in a little island all his own.

Mr. Weiss's bushy eyebrows arched a bit, surprised, but he said nothing. When he turned toward the chalkboard, I saw him smile. It was almost a grin.

19

By the time class was over, my heart had slowed down to normal. But I felt very tired, exhausted even. I also felt relieved. No more catering to Kevin, flattering his pathetic ego. Telling him how great he was. The worst had happened, Kevin was out of the play. At least it had been my decision. When the bell rang, I stood up straight, and walked to the door with dignity.

As I was passing Mr. Weiss's desk, he said, "Oh. Zainab. That phone call was Jenny's mom. She's home from the hospital, in case you'd like to pay her a visit."

"How is she?"

"She'll be fine. How about you?"

"I'm okay. But, Mr. Weiss?"

"Hmmm?"

"I don't think I'll be able to do the play. I kicked Kevin out."

His eyebrow arched, and he grinned. "Really? What if you changed to another play?"

"Now? Do I have to?"

Mr. Weiss puffed out his cheeks and blew out a long slow breath. "Well, Zainab. You don't have to, but without the play, Mackenzie King will lose for sure. And what's more, Kevin will think he won. He'll think that you can't do a play without him."

"But I can. I just don't want to."

Mr. Weiss shrugged. "That's not the way he'll see it."

I clenched my fists, the heat rising. He was right. Everyone would say that Kevin had won. For myself, I didn't really care anymore. They could think what they liked — I knew what I was. But Jenny. She'd lost so much. For her sake, I'd like to win.

"Okay, Mr. Weiss. After recess I'll call for new auditions. We'll see what happens."

"Oh, and Zainab. I really wish you'd do something from your culture. I'll tell you a secret. The judges have seen lots of plays like *The Emperor's New Clothes*. I'm sure they'd love something fresh and different."

"But there's no time. We've only got six weeks."

"Well, it's up to you. It's just a suggestion."

Why did everyone want me to do something from my culture? Our stories just didn't translate well. Look at the way Premini had reacted to that hadith I'd told her. I'd loved the story, Premini hadn't. And yet nobody really liked *The Emperor's New Clothes*. Even my confidence in it was gone. I wanted to start fresh, put the disastrous past behind me.

The only good thing about Kevin's being out of the play was that, being in Mackenzie King, he couldn't go to one of the other house leagues and join their play. It was my play or no play for him. But what was going to stop him from telling the other leagues what we were doing? Nothing at all. Maybe it would be best to do another play.

I said goodbye to Mr. Weiss and hustled outside. I had a germ of an idea I'd have to discuss with Premini and maybe Jenny too.

When I talked to Premini at recess she told me she was willing to be the lead in the play, whatever story I did. With her as the lead we had a chance.

At the new auditions, there were a few more people than I'd expected. Premini and the geometry twins were there but so were ten others. They were quiet, in-the-middle kids, not popular, not picked on. I'd never really noticed them before. One of the girls, Delilah, pretty with dark brown hair, signed up and said, "You know, I'm really glad you gave it to Kevin. It was awful the way he treated Jenny."

I smiled at her, and she smiled back. I had an idea. "Do you want to sign a card for her?"

"Sure!"

Everyone at the auditions signed. The card looked almost crowded with signatures now.

Delilah asked, "What play are we auditioning for?"

"Well, um, at this point we really don't have a play," I confessed. "I still have to write it. But audition anyway, okay? Show me what you can do, and I'll keep that in mind when the play is finalized and I'm casting the characters. We're really short of time, so I have to do it this way."

There were a few murmurs. A bit of confusion. But they seemed to understand, and the auditions began.

Delilah wasn't the greatest actress, but at this point I wasn't going to be too picky. Three of them couldn't act at all, and didn't want to. They ended up with backstage duties — lights, costumes and curtains. We had six weeks to pull this off. After everyone had auditioned I stood up, my clipboard at my side, and said, "I want to warn all of you that this play isn't going to be easy. There's not many of us, so we'll each have to work extra hard. But I'm planning to win, and if we don't, it won't be because we didn't try. But before you sign up, you should know that things might get a little nasty. Kevin might bug you all for joining up with me. If you feel like you'd rather not cross Kevin, I'll understand and you can leave now. But once you've joined, please don't back out." I paused.

All eyes were steady on me, determined. Nobody shuffled their feet or looked away. I smiled. "Well then, this is the year we'll break the curse of Mackenzie King. Are you with me?"

They didn't quite cheer, but they did nod and some even said aloud a hearty "Yes."

I walked home feeling pretty good. We were a dedicated bunch, even if we were few in number. And being few, I was coming to realize, wasn't so bad. The fewer there were, the easier they would be to control. They might actually listen without too many arguments and yet with the occasional discussion. And there was no Kevin to disrupt things. We had something to work with, and even if we didn't win, we would make Mackenzie King proud.

I got home and prayed Zuhr. Then I prayed the extra prayers, the nafil, that I'd promised God. To thank Him for making Jenny okay.

When I finished, I put my hands together to ask for one more thing. Let us win the play competition. I really wanted to. To be totally honest, it wasn't only for Jenny. I wanted it for me, too.

I told my mother that Jenny was home from the hospital and asked if I could go over after supper. She said that was fine but I had to finish my homework first. I sat down on my bed and started the grammar exercises.

Layla came and leaned against the door-frame, her arms folded.

I tried to ignore her but she was staring at me. Finally I said, "What is it? What do you want?"

She came in and closed the door behind her. "Jenny didn't just have an accident. She tried to kill herself."

I dropped my pen and it rolled off the bed. While I bent to get it, I tried to think of what to say. "Uh, what do you mean? Of course she just had an accident." I winced. I didn't sound convincing even to myself.

Layla sat down on my bed. "Come off it, Zainab. You're a lousy liar."

I sighed. "Fine. She tried to kill herself. It was her phoning that night. She'd just taken an overdose of pills. She was calling for help."

"I'm telling Ami. You're not supposed to pray for someone who's committed suicide."

"But she didn't commit it, she only tried. It's like a cry for help. I'm just trying to help her."

"I'm still telling Ami."

"Please, Layla, don't. I'm not doing anything wrong. I'm just going to visit her, to see how she's doing. I'm giving her this card I made. That's all."

"You don't need to visit her, she's not a Muslim."

"What do you mean? Don't you know that visiting the sick is one of the duties of a Muslim? It's in the hadiths."

She avoided my eyes. "Um, yeah, but doesn't that only apply to Muslims?"

I was really puzzled. "It applies to everyone. Don't you remember that woman who hated the Prophet, peace be upon him, so much she used to throw garbage on him everyday? And then one day she was sick and didn't come. The Prophet, peace be upon him, went to visit her, to find out if she was okay."

She wrinkled her nose. "Oh, yeah."

"She wasn't Muslim."

"Yeah, yeah, but you're not telling Ami the truth."

"Jenny did fall. I did find her unconscious. I didn't lie. I just know Ami'd be upset if she knew the whole story. I have to help Jenny. No one else is."

"Okay, okay. I guess I won't say anything. But don't take too long."

I nodded and got back to my homework. I finished before supper and, right after, I skipped out the door.

Layla had to clean the kitchen by herself that night, my mother said.

As I got closer and closer to Jenny's house, I got more and more nervous. What did one say to their best friend who's just tried to kill herself?

Her mother let me in. I guess she didn't bother getting dressed up unless there was a guy involved. She had on a bathrobe with coffee stains. A cigarette dangled from the corner of her mouth. Without make-up she looked bland, like boiled macaroni without the cheese. She gave me a hostile look when she answered the door. I asked if I could see Jenny.

She left me waiting out on the cold step while she looked me over from head to toe, then finally nodded. I followed her in. She shuffled into the kitchen, plunked down into a chair and picked up her newspaper. There was a cup of black coffee beside her.

I hesitated only a moment. I didn't know which was Jenny's room, but I wasn't going to ask. I walked softly into the hallway, trying not to let the floor creak and disturb Mrs. — Ms. — Roberts.

On the right, I came to what could only be Jenny's room. A profusion of pink roses on pink wallpaper, faded pink ruffled curtains, a dusty pink dresser with a pink-tinted mirror, a pink bed with a dingy pink ruffled canopy. The bed would have fit a five year old nicely, but Jenny's feet touched the footboard, and she'd have to bend to see her face in that pink-tinted mirror.

She was sitting up in bed, leaning her head against the pink satin headboard, staring vacantly at the ceiling.

When she saw me, she lifted her head straight and half-smiled. "Hi, Zainab." Her voice broke, like she wanted to cry. Her eyes were as pink as her comforter and her eyelids were swollen, but free of makeup. She looked clean, fresh, new. She looked like the old Jenny, but pale.

She asked me to close the door. I did, then sat down on the foot of her bed. Trying not to stare at the comforter. Like everything else, it needed washing.

I said, "How are you doing?"

She looked down at the comforter, twisting the material between her fingers. "Okay, I guess. I heard what you did for me. Thanks for coming. I tried calling you. It was so hard. I could hardly manage to dial, and then when I finally got through, someone thought I was drunk, and started yelling at me."

I winced. "That's my older sister, Layla."

Jenny didn't say anything.

I gave her the card. She smiled, her eyes shiny with tears. "Thanks. Oh thanks so much. You don't know what it means to me."

"It's nothing." I looked down at my hands and noticed my nails needed cutting. I had to ask her. I had to know. But it wasn't easy. I took a deep breath and said, "Why, Jenny? Why did you do it?"

She shrugged. "I know it was stupid. After I swallowed the pills . . . I changed my mind. I was afraid. I didn't know who to call. And my mom, we'd had this huge fight. I just thought it would be easier."

"And Kevin?"

Her eyes filled with tears and her mouth twisted. "Oh, God, Kevin!"

I leaned forward and hugged her. She buried her face into my neck, reminding me of Waleed. I patted her back, saying, "Don't cry, Jenny. You've cried enough to last a lifetime." It was something my mother always said to comfort me.

It worked. She smiled a little and sat up straight, grabbing a tissue from the box on her bedside table.

"That's it. Chin up, old girl. Things aren't that bad. Besides, you should have seen the way I handled Kevin. I bet he's sorry he ever messed with you."

Her baby blue eyes were round and huge as she gaped at me. "What?"

I told her, but not about the two minutes of silence.

She listened to the whole story without interrupting. Then she shook her head sadly. "Oh, Zainab. I wish you hadn't done that."

"He deserved it."

She shook her head.

"But, Jenny, after all he did to you. The pictures and everything."

She gaped at me. "You know about the pictures?"

I nodded. "Why did you let him take them?"

She sighed. "I love him so much. I just couldn't say no. It was stupid, but I trusted him."

"But why? I told you not to."

She looked down again at her fingers, twisting the comforter into a tighter and tighter knot. She whispered, "He told me he loved me."

I wanted to shake her, slap her, knock some sense into her.

I said, "Well, anyway, I kicked him out of the play. I was thinking of doing a story from my culture instead of *The Emperor's New Clothes*, and I was wondering what you think of the idea."

"You didn't have to kick him out of the play."

"But I did it for you. You'll see. We'll show him we can do it without him."

"I can't. I don't even think I can face everyone at school."

"What do you mean?"

Jenny took a deep breath. "I'm thinking of leaving Glen Hollow."

My jaw dropped open. "But, Jenny, you can't leave."

Tears splashed down her cheeks. "I have to. How can I . . . how can I ever face them? They all know. By now, it's all over the school. And how can I go there, seeing Kevin every day, knowing how he feels, still loving him anyway?"

"But I need you." Tears stung my eyes, but I laughed inside at my foolishness. I was here to cheer Jenny up — instead, I was crying myself.

"Oh, Zainab. I'm sorry."

"But, Jenny, you'll see. Everyone will talk for a while but then they'll stop. Besides, I have a plan. How you can get even with Kevin."

Jenny shook her head slowly. "I don't want to get even. I don't want to hurt him at all."

"But after all he's done to you . . ."

"I can't help it. No matter what, I still love him. I'm sorry."

I felt like smacking her again. I stood up, my hands on my hips. "Fine. If you're really sorry, you won't go. You owe me, Jenny."

"Zainab, don't."

"I saved your life. You owe me."

"What do you want from me?"

"I want you to come back to school for six weeks. Until this stupid play is done. Then you'll see. Don't run away. Face Kevin. Face everyone."

Jenny hid her face in her hands, sobbing wretchedly. "I can't. Don't ask me to."

I put my hand on her shoulder. "Stop crying, Jenny. You're making the tissue company rich."

She laughed again, through her tears, but didn't stop crying.

I said, "Don't you see, Jenny? Running away's not the answer."

She lifted her head. "But I'm not running away. Really, I'm not. When I took the pills, that was running away. Now I'm leaving, because I have to. I have no other choice."

It was like the hadith. That story of the man who'd killed those people. Jenny hadn't killed anyone, but like that guy, she had to make a fresh start. Put the past behind her.

"Where will you go?" I asked.

She wiped her eyes and dropped the tissue in the waste basket. "I talked to my mother. We both agreed it would be for the best. I'm going to go stay with my grandfather on his farm."

I could picture her on a farm. Riding horses, tossing hay. I asked, "When are you going?"

"In a few days."

"I'm going to miss you."

Tears filled her eyes again. "Oh, Zainab. I'm going to miss you too."

I felt warm. Like she'd hugged me.

"I'll write."

"You'd better!" I warned.

There was an awkward silence. I stood up. "I'd better go. It's getting late."

She nodded.

I hugged her. She smelled like soap. "Bye, Jenny."

"Bye, Zainab. And thanks."

"Sure."

20

By the time I got home, I'd decided that I'd definitely write a play based on a Muslim story. But not the hadith I'd originally thought of doing.

I called up Premini. "What about this story?" I said, and briefly summarized it for her over the phone.

Premini laughed. "I like that one. Yeah, why not? We could do it. We've got enough people."

"Who do you want to be, the emperor or the sheikh?"

"The emperor will be tougher. Yeah, I guess I'll be the emperor. Besides, I've always wanted to play royalty."

I laughed. "Sounds good. I'm going to sit down and write the play. I'll work all weekend. See you on Monday."

I started working on the play right then.

It was almost time for bed but I had too much work to do to think about sleeping. Layla came in while I was still writing and asked what I was doing.

I told her. "It's the play. It's not exactly a hadith. It's a Muslim story. Based on something from the Quran."

She grinned. It lit up her face, showing off her pearly white teeth and perfect skin. She really was beautiful. "That's great. I'm so glad you decided to listen to me."

I didn't correct her. I didn't tell her that she'd had nothing to do with it.

She looked over my papers. I hoped she couldn't read what I'd written. She said, "Maybe I should give your faults now, so that I won't disturb you later."

Surprisingly enough, the list was getting shorter. Arrogance was gone, and so was laziness. I guess all the volunteering in the kitchen had paid off. Or maybe it was just that Layla was in a good mood because of the play.

I spent most of Saturday with my nose in Islamic history books. It wasn't as boring as it sounds. It turns out that Jehangir, the emperor in the story I'd decided on, was the father of Shah Jehan, the guy who built the world-famous Taj Mahal. Even Mr. Weiss knows about the Taj Mahal. It's one of the Seven Wonders of the World. And Jehangir's father was Akbar. A real weirdo. He made up his own religion, and said that he was God. What a power trip.

Jehangir was Akbar's son from a Hindu woman. Premini would find that interesting.

I decided to refer to the sheikh in the story as "the alim." Alim means learned one, and he certainly was.

The word sheikh has too many connotations. It carries an image of a guy who runs around on camels and has lots of women, like in the Valentino movies. Sheikh actually means scholar, but few people know that.

One problem was that, like most of history, the story didn't end in a neat and tidy way. It was one of those long, arduous struggles. Although the alim did come out victorious in the end, it wasn't in one single climactic scene, like in the movies, where the villain dies or comes to his senses. It was only after years of sacrifice and struggle that the emperor saw the error of his ways.

I only had twenty minutes for the play. Twenty minutes for the alim to emerge victorious. And another problem was that Jehangir wasn't quite as bad as I wanted him to be. He wasn't evil; just kind of a bully.

But I figured out a way to concentrate the story into three acts. Perfect. The best plays were three acts. I'd read that somewhere. There would be an initial scene where Jehangir has the alim brought before him on trumped-up charges, because he's afraid that this learned man is getting too popular, and might lead the people in a revolt.

Jehangir has a fabulous throne, studded with jewels and precious gems, and whoever comes before him has to bow down, and kiss the floor in front of the throne.

Jehangir wanted people to kiss the floor, and Kevin expected everyone to kiss his . . . um, never mind. I guess things weren't that different back then, only on a grander scale. Seems everybody was too scared to tell Jehangir off. All the Islamic scholars went along. Nobody dared speak out, even when the emperor was doing something that was obviously wrong.

The second scene would be in a dungeon. The Gwalior Fort prison where Jehangir had the alim locked up for more than a year.

I was tempted to change history — give Jehangir a heart attack so he could keel over at the right, climactic moment. Foaming at the mouth in a mad frenzy. But history wouldn't co-operate. He didn't die till long after this incident.

I called Premini. To ask her what she thought. I also wanted to see if she'd be offended by anything that was happening in the play.

Premini said, "About that bowing down stuff. What's the big deal?"

"As Muslims, we're only supposed to bow before God."

"Why?"

What a question! It was obvious. But how could I explain?

"Well?" said Premini.

"It's a matter of submission. The only one we're supposed to submit to is God. By bowing down, you're putting your face, the highest part of your body, on the floor. You're humbling yourself. But you're not supposed to do that for people. No person is worth it. Because no one is that much better than any other. We only do that for God."

"Humph. Then what were you chasing after Kevin for? Weren't you humbling yourself before him?"

"Yeah. I guess so. I didn't realize."

Premini went on. "Well, you weren't the only one. Jenny was at it, too."

I didn't say anything, but I was thinking how the play might mean something to other kids who ended up "bowing down" for the wrong reasons.

Layla came in just then and gave me a dirty look for being on the phone so long. I said my goodbyes and hung up.

On Sunday night, Layla sank down on her bed. "Well, you've been keeping things from our parents, you still take too much time in the shower, you interfere in Seema and Waleed's fights, you took off to Jenny's house without proper permission, you've been leaving the lids off the toothpaste, shampoo, baby oil. Oh, and you've been forgetting to put a new roll of toilet paper on the roller when it runs out. I went in the washroom after you a couple of times and found it empty."

I'd closed my eyes to check on the state of my brick wall, but now I opened them again. "That's it?"

Layla frowned, "Well, you have improved. I'll be the first to admit it."

I closed my eyes and examined my wall again. It still had a few imperfections but it seemed pretty solid now. I rather liked it.

I opened my eyes, a smile on my face. "Is that really all there is? Isn't there anything else?"

"Nope. That's it."

"Well then. Thanks very much, Layla, I've really appreciated your help, but I guess I won't be needing these self-improvement sessions anymore."

She looked alarmed. "What do you mean? Do you think you're so perfect that you don't still need to improve?"

"Not at all. I know I'm not perfect. I never will be. I can't even hope to be. Perfection belongs to Allah. But if these are my faults, then they're faults I can live with."

"You mean they don't bother you?"

"No."

"You just don't like criticism."

"It's not that. There are people who murder, steal, rape, and do all kinds of bad things. If I leave the lids off things and interfere in some fights and other minor faults, I can live with that. I'll still try to improve and remember to put the lids on but, after all, I can't be perfect. I must have something to ask Allah to forgive me for."

She sniffed. "Well, if you think there's no room for improvement then I feel sorry for you. You needn't worry. I'll never bother you with a self-improvement plan again. I can see you don't appreciate it."

"I'm sorry you feel that way, Layla. I do appreciate what you've done."

"If you appreciated it, you'd want it to continue. Why did I bother? You really are hopeless. Humph."

"Wait a minute, you're the one who said all I had to do was ask you to stop and you would."

"I at least thought you'd wait till you really had improved." She crossed her arms and turned her back on me.

The old guilt was back. The old self-doubts. Layla didn't approve. But darn it! I did. I had improved. If she didn't think so, even though she'd just said so, that was too bad. I didn't have time to bother with her. I liked my wall. That should be enough. It was enough. She could go build her own. I had a play to write.

I turned away, and started working on the play again. I don't know when Layla left the room. I don't even know when she went to sleep. I was too busy to notice.

I finished the play that very night. It wasn't until midnight, but I finished it. Maybe it was because of Jenny, or maybe it was because I'd been thinking a lot over the past few weeks. I knew exactly what I wanted to say. When I was done, I was quite pleased.

I gave it to Premini to read the next day. I watched her eyebrows arch in surprise, and the way her thin brown lips moved as she read the words. Her yellowish face glowed. She'd forgotten I was there.

She blinked when she was done. Then she looked at me. "It's good. We might win."

"I hope so," I said. But we still had a lot of work to do.

I needn't have worried about Kevin harassing the kids who'd joined the play. He avoided me and he avoided anybody that had anything to do with me. I avoided him too. I figured he thought of us as a bunch of losers who didn't stand a chance of winning.

Every afternoon, I prayed two extra nafil after my Zuhr prayer and begged God to let us win. It was bribery but I knew we needed all the help we could get.

It turned out that I couldn't just be the director. The second major character, the alim, had to be me. My costume was easy. I took one of my dad's kurthas, a long robe, and a topi, a prayer cap, and tucked my ponytail into the shirt.

Every day for six weeks we rehearsed at least once a day, sometimes twice. And toward the end, Mr. Weiss gave us time off class to get in an extra rehearsal.

I wasn't the only director. I encouraged anyone who had something to say to say it. As a result, we all directed each other. When I said one of my lines with the wrong expression, everyone jumped on me. And it was the same for all of them. But it was friendly. Everyone knew we were only trying to make the play better.

Gosh, we worked hard. It got to be routine. I knew Premini's lines as well as she knew them herself, and sometimes, while she was saying them, my mind wandered and I looked around at all the intense, eager faces, hoping I wouldn't let them down.

We were counting on winning. What if we didn't? What if the play wasn't as good as I, we, thought it was? The other kids had told me how much they liked it. But what if they'd only said it so I'd give them a part? Or to be nice?

Whenever these thoughts whirred around in my mind I just had to tell myself to stop being dumb. The play was good. The kids did like it. And so would the audience.

It was exhausting. All the work on the sets, the costumes, the lighting. The rehearsals, till I dreamed every night I was saying my lines. And as the contest drew closer and closer, the dreams got weirder and weirder. One night I wasn't the alim, but Jehangir, and I couldn't remember his lines, and Premini and all the actors were staring at me, and the whole school was staring at me, and I tried to read my part from the script, but the letters were blurry and no one could hear me. And one night, I'm ashamed to say, I dreamed that everyone was in costume but me. I was standing there on stage in my pyjamas. I was so embarrassed, but no one seemed to notice.

But at least without Layla's self-improvement sessions I got a lot more sleep. She was still sulking. But I was too busy to worry about her.

I have to admit though, the first few days were hard. She didn't talk to me once. She relayed all her instructions through Waleed or Seema — "Tell Zainab to move in her chair, I can't get past" or, "Tell Zainab to pick up her coat, it's in the way." Even when I was standing right there. But there's a hadith that a Muslim can only be mad at another Muslim for three days. So after three days, Layla would tell me herself to get out of the way, or pass the roti. Things like that.

But she'd also add comments like, "Oh, but you think you're perfect. You think you're just fine the way you are. You think you don't need improving." At first I wanted to answer, but I stopped myself. The more I answered, the more she would know she was getting to me.

If I hadn't been so occupied with the play, I think I would have given in during the first week. Asked her to continue the self-improvement sessions. But that would've been a mistake. I was enjoying not having them. And as the days went by, it got easier and easier. I cared less and less what she thought. I really was okay. A pretty straight and strong wall, if I did say so myself.

Finally, it was the day of the competition. At fajr, I made extra prayers, asking God again to let us win.

21

They were like a field of sunflowers facing me, the sun. How would I ever be good enough to please them? Mr. Weiss grinned, nodding encouragement. Kevin scowled, glaring. The judges sat behind their table, pens poised, ready to scratch down their comments, their judgements. One of them, a woman, stifled a yawn.

We were the last ones to perform. Laurier, Pearson, Macdonald, all had gone before, and they had been good. Laurier had done a few scenes from *Romeo and Juliet*. Fine, except that Juliet had a bit of a cold, and said, "Womeo, Womeo, wherefore ard dou Womeo?"

I don't know why everyone always does the balcony scene. I like the scene where they first meet, and Romeo tries to steal a kiss.

Pearson did a piece from *The Wizard of Oz*. The scene where Dorothy throws the water on the witch and she melts. It was quite good, but I kept comparing it to the movie. Here the witch just ended up collapsing in a heap, instead of really melting down to nothing, like in the movie.

Macdonald did *Cinderella*, a modern version. Where Cinderella is dying for a pair of Lucky jeans to go to the school dance. I could relate.

And now, finally, it was our turn.

I stood on the stage and spoke loud and clear, despite the butterflies in my stomach. "A long time ago, there lived a courageous man who dared to stand up to a tyrannical ruler. His name was Sheikh Ahmad Sirhindi, and he was an alim — a wise man. The alim was born on May 26th in the year 1564, during the reign of the first Moghul emperor, Akbar." Then I paused, for effect, and said, "Akbar was an idiot."

How they laughed! I waited till they quieted and went on. I told them how Akbar had persecuted the Muslims, ridiculing them, even though he was supposed to be Muslim himself. How most of the Muslims in his court changed their Islamic names to something less offensive to his "highness." And I told of how the alim had worked quietly and patiently for many years, teaching the people what it meant to be a Muslim. A real Muslim.

I paused for breath and noticed a peculiar thing. The lady judge was sitting up and listening. And Kevin had stopped scowling. Now he just looked worried. Figuring that was a good sign, I relaxed, smiled, and took a few steps toward the audience.

"But eventually all tyrants die," I said, looking pointedly at Kevin. "And so Akbar died too, and his son, Jehangir, took the throne. But Jehangir, too, was afraid of the alim. There were rumors in the court that one day this quiet man's popularity would lead to a revolt. Now Jehangir had a wise son, Shah Jehan, who liked the alim and told his father not to worry. But there were others, among them the court chamberlain, who whispered in the ear of the emperor — false, evil tales of the alim's ambition and growing power. So the day came when Jehangir summoned the wise man to his court in Agra." I nodded at the boy in charge of the curtains, then turned back to the audience. "This is the point where we begin our play." And I ducked out of sight behind the curtains as they started to open.

Emperor Jehangir (Premini) sat on a beautiful "throne," studded with precious gems (rhinestones and plastic). She had to sit carefully or the cardboard would come off, revealing the chair beneath. Shah Jehan (Delilah) stood beside her. The chamberlain (Dan) sat on a footstool, lower than the emperor. All three were wearing turbans, but Premini wore hers like it was part of her head, like she wore one every day. Whereas Delilah looked slightly uncomfortable, and Dan held his head at a peculiar angle to keep his turban balanced, glancing up every now and then to make sure it was still there.

Shah Jehan began, "O my Emperor father, you will have patience with the alim? He is a simple man, not used to the ways of the court."

Jehangir stroked his chin in a pensive, emperor-like fashion. "We shall see what we shall see. Send him in, Chamberlain."

With a sneer, the chamberlain escorted me out of the shadows to center stage. For a moment, I just stood there. Then he said, "Bow before the emperor. It is customary to kiss the floor before the throne."

I cocked my head (and my turban almost fell off). "Customary? Customary for whom? I know of no such custom practiced by the blessed Prophet, peace be upon him."

The chamberlain stood with his mouth gaping, as if at my nerve. I was proud of Dan! And Jehangir sat up. Premini's voice range out like a true ruler. "In my great father's time, it was customary for anyone entering the throne room to kiss the floor. I demand that you do so."

Here I shook my head. "I cannot. Such prostration is only permitted to Allah, my Lord and Creator. It is not fitting that I humble myself before another man."

Jehangir said, "I'm not just any man. I am your emperor. This is inexcusable. You will kiss the floor or I will throw you into Gwalior Fort prison. Make your choice!"

I looked at Premini with as much dignity as I could muster. "Under your title and fancy clothes, you are a man, just like me. Do you not see that what you ask is against every principle of Islam? And yet you call yourself Muslim. Do you forget the story of Abraham, peace be upon him, when he argued with the king?"

Jehangir knitted his brow. "That story eludes me.

Recite it for me."

"There was once a king who argued with Abraham, peace be upon him, about who was greater, himself or God, even though God had been kind enough to make him a king. Abraham told him that God had the power of life and death. The king said that he too had the power of life and death, in that he could kill anyone if he chose. Then Abraham said, 'Verily, God causes the sun to rise in the east. Can you make it rise in the west?' At that, the king was furious, because he had no answer.

"You see, O Emperor, that king demanded Abraham's submission, just as you have demanded mine. Abraham refused. And so do I."

Jehangir smiled. "So then, you have made your choice." He turned to the chamberlain. "Take him to Gwalior Fort prison."

Shah Jehan cried, "Father, no." Jehangir raised a hand to silence him and Shah Jehan was silent. The curtains closed.

End of Act I.

Quickly, we brought out the change of set. Prison bars, and drab prison furnishings. Carefully removing the carboard-covered throne, to be used in the last scenes. I muddied my face a bit, put on a tattered turban and kurtha. I slipped on grey paper chains, and we were ready. The curtains opened on Act II.

I sat on the floor of the stage. The chamberlain escorted Shah Jehan in. The prince looked at the unfamiliar surroundings of the prison. The chamberlain led him across the stage, stepping over foreign objects, a sneer of distaste on his face. His nose was covered with a piece of cloth. He said, "Watch your step, Your Majesty. This is no place for a Moghul prince!"

Shah Jehan said, "It's no place for a man of God, either! Ah, there's the alim."

Getting to my feet, I said, "Prince Shah Jehan. It is good to see you."

Shah Jehan smiled. "I've come to see that you are treated well. I would have come sooner, but my father would not permit it. Are you well, Alim? Do you want for anything?"

"I am content."

The chamberlain scowled. Shah Jehan looked worried. "I have come to beg you to relent. Submission to my father is not so bad. Under the circumstances, God would forgive you. You do not have to suffer like this."

I smiled. "My imprisonment is tolerable. The guards have come to like me and I've had the chance to teach so many I would not normally have met. Even some of the guards have become my students. In a way, it has been a blessing."

"Don't you wish to leave this prison?"

"Of course. But I will not kiss your father's floor to do so. I will not bow my will to him, just to be free. What kind of freedom is that? I'd rather have a prison of my own choosing."

Shah Jehan said, "The prostration does not mean anything. It's just a custom. You can still believe in your heart what you wish."

"That's fine for some, but not for me. There comes a time when you must stand up and say, 'No. I will not submit to you. You are not worthy of it. I am just as good. Even if I have no throne, or crown on my head. Even if my clothes are not fancy.'"

Shah Jehan cried, "But it hurts me to see you imprisoned like this. I would see you free."

I said, "Then pray for me. Pray that God softens the emperor's heart. That is what I pray for. And do not lose hope."

The chamberlain tugged on Shah Jehan's sleeve. "Come, my prince, you have done your best. He is too stubborn to listen."

Shah Jehan was reluctantly led away. The curtains closed. The end of Act II.

Quickly, we replaced the furnishings for the throne room, and Premini sat down. Shah Jehan took a position by her side, and the chamberlain sat on the footstool. The curtains opened.

Shah Jehan said, "O my Emperor father. You have imprisoned the alim for more than a year now, can't you let him go? It is clear he does not care for your throne. He only wants to teach people."

"How do you know he doesn't want my throne? The people rise up in revolt. I know he is behind it."

The chamberlain said, "Yes indeed, sire, he even charms the guards of Gwalior Fort prison. Perhaps he means to turn them against you, too. To win his escape that way."

Shah Jehan said, "Nonsense."

Jehangir nodded. "I agree with my son. The alim knows the price of his freedom is small. A simple prostration. Why would he try to set my own guards, whom I pay well, against me? It is the masses, the people, who worry me. The alim is their hero. He can incite them to rebellion . . ."

Shah Jehan said, "The people rise up to protest his imprisonment. If you let him go, they would have no reason to rise up. He is well-liked everywhere. And yes, by the guards of the prison, too. Doesn't that say something about his character?"

Jehangir said, "Well, I've told him what he must do if he wants his release. It is not my fault he is too stubborn to kiss the floor. At this point, I'd even settle for a bow. But he must submit."

Shah Jehan threw up his arms in frustration. The chamberlain sat up. "Sire, I have an idea. Why not trick him into it? Gather all your courtiers. Then bring the alim to the throne room, but block the entrance in some way, leaving only a tunnel that he must crawl through. When he emerges on hands and knees, I will declare that he has bowed down."

Shah Jehan said, "No, father. You wouldn't!"

Jehangir stroked his chin and smiled, a slow wicked grin. He said, "Shah Jehan, you gather the courtiers. Chamberlain, put up the barricade. Set up the tunnel, then go and get the alim."

Jehangir walked to the front of the stage, facing the audience. Being backstage, I couldn't see his face, but the effect on the audience was profound. All eyes were fixed on him. No one stirred as he said, "We shall see what comes of it." Jehangir backed away just as the curtains closed on Act III, Scene 1.

Rushing as always, we set up the last scene.

The other actors gathered around Jehangir. Shah Jehan looked glum. The barricade was brought out — a wall with a small opening for the tunnel, a curved piece of cardboard, large enough for me to pass through. Then the chamberlain and I went behind it and again the curtains opened, the audience stopped whispering. All was quiet.

Jehangir asked Shah Jehan, "Well? Where is the alim?"

From where I stood, I could peek around the barricade without being seen by the audience. Shah Jehan had bent down to peer through the tunnel. "He comes, father." Then he returned to stand beside Jehangir.

Shah Jehan was smiling. The audience was waiting expectantly. Time for the climax.

Carefully, I got down on my behind, and entered the tunnel, wiggling my way through. And emerging. Feet first. Not head bowed. I looked up innocently at Jehangir. And waited for the audience's reaction.

They laughed. As a great wave of relief swept through me.

I sat up on my knees and watched Jehangir. This was the moment that I'd been worried about all along. Could Premini make the change in the emperor convincing?

She had to take Jehangir from anger to resignation. With no dialogue to help her.

She stood up, oh so slowly. On her face, rage mixed with wonderment was clearly visible. Her fists were clenched. She took a deliberate turn around the stage, circling me. Utter silence was all around her. It seemed the audience held their breath, and all those on stage too. So much of the emotion she conveyed was in her shoulders. At first she had them hunched high and tight, but now, ever so gradually, they were relaxing. Slowly, the warring emotions on Premini's face settled. It was as if we could read her thoughts. Without words, she let us know what was going through her head.

Truly amazing. The sign of a real actor. Anger gave way to respect, then even a little humor. At one point, Premini glanced my way, and smiled as if in spite of herself. And then finally the emotion I'd been waiting for. Resignation. She didn't shrug. She didn't need to. But you could see, by the slope of those shoulders, that Jehangir knew he was outwitted. And he accepted it. There was a collective sigh. A releasing of breaths held as the moment passed.

Jehangir sat back down. And addressed the alim, as if that's why he'd called him there in the first place. "Now, Alim, you were speaking of the traditions of the Prophet, peace be upon him. In my father's time, we strayed far from these traditions. Perhaps it is time we corrected that. I would have you tell me more."

Slowly the curtains began to close, although we, the actors, continued to speak our lines. It was clear that though the play was over, the story went on.

The curtains were fully closed, at last. But it wasn't over. There was applause, more than what would be considered polite. In fact, it seemed enthusiastic. I nodded to one of the backstage crew, and he flicked on the house lights.

As I stepped out onto the stage once more, the applause, which had died down somewhat, flared up again. And nobody, not even Kevin, booed.

I waited till there was quiet, then said, "The story of Alim, Sheikh Ahmad Sirhindi does not end here. Jehangir released the Alim from Gwalior Fort prison, but asked him to remain with his armed forces for quite some time. Jehangir did this to convince himself that the alim truly wasn't trying to take his throne. The alim used the opportunity to teach the soldiers, the captains and whomever would listen, more about what it was to be Muslim. When Jehangir was finally satisfied that the alim didn't want his throne, he let him go.

"The alim had a profound influence on Jehangir, but even more on his son. When Jehangir died, and Shah Jehan became the third Moghul emperor, he abolished the ceremonial prostration before the throne. It was Shah Jehan who built the world-famous Taj Mahal and the Shalimar gardens. But the alim never lived to see them. He died on December 10th, 1624, two years before Shah Jehan became emperor."

The audience began clapping again. Smiling and clapping. Only Kevin sat with his arms crossed, a big scowl on his face.

The judges were busy writing down notes.

I ducked into the curtains. Premini came up beside me. I whispered, "Do you think they liked it?"

She shrugged. "They're clapping, aren't they? Don't worry about it. We were good."

"Do you really think so? Did I say my lines okay?"

She grinned, patting me on the back. "You were fine. What about me?"

"Great."

Mr. Weiss appeared backstage, urging us all to take seats in the audience, along with the participants from the other house league plays.

About ten minutes later, when we could hardly sit still a moment longer, he parted the curtains and stepped onto the stage.

"On behalf of the judges," he began, "I'd like to thank all the participants. Everyone did a wonderful job and everyone deserves to win. Let's have a round of applause for all the people who worked so hard on the plays."

There was some hearty laughter. Now I really couldn't sit still. Kevin was watching me, a smug look on his face. He whispered, "You lost, Zainy! What a lousy play!"

I whispered back, "Shut up!"

He sneered and looked away.

The judges started walking toward the stage. They looked very serious.

The woman's high heels clicked loudly as she went up the stairs to the stage, followed by the two men. There was a hush across the gym. The principal cleared his throat, "Ahem. As usual it was a very hard decision. All the participants did a wonderful job. But this year the winner was outstanding. The winner showed great courage in producing a play that was truly original, in an entertaining and creative manner."

I held my breath. It sounded as though he was talking about us. But I wouldn't believe it. Not until he said it.

The principal continued, "We as the judges feel that we must reward such originality with none other than the first prize. The winner of this year's house league drama competition is . . ." Then the principal looked right at me. "Mackenzie King."

I almost thought my ears were playing tricks on me, and he'd really said Laurier. But no. Premini was hugging me, jumping up and down, Delilah was shaking my hand, pumping it hard. Mr. Weiss was saying something, his moustache stretched from cheek to cheek in a huge grin. Vaguely, I heard Kevin yelling, "NO! No!"

There was a buzz in my ears like a thousand bees. Somehow I got on stage, and looked out over the audience. Almost everyone was smiling, and the ones that weren't didn't matter.

We'd done it. We'd actually broken the curse of Mackenzie King.

The principal said, "I think this victory is especially important since it marks the first time Mackenzie King has ever won the competition. Congratulations, Zainab Chaudry, Premini Gupta, and the rest of the cast. Keep up the good work."

I waited for the applause to die down and then said, "I'd really like to thank a few people who've helped us so much. Premini. You really are an emperor. We couldn't have done it without you." Kevin's face grew red when I said that.

"And thanks to all the kids who worked on the show. You did an excellent job. And special thanks to Jenny Roberts, who can't be with us today. This one's for you, Jenny."

The applause was really loud now. Most were even smiling.

It was better than I could have dreamed.

22

With the play finished, and Mackenzie King sure winners of the house league competitions, school returned to its normal routine. But for me a lot of things had changed.

I had friends. Friends who joked with me and asked me how I did on my math test.

There was Premini. She really was a lot better than I'd imagined. Over time, I didn't even have to be careful of what I said. It came automatically. I knew the kinds of things that would upset her and I just avoided them. Sometimes she'd make a remark that bugged me. When it bugged me enough, I told her. At first she'd say I was too sensitive and couldn't I take a joke. But then she'd never repeat the remark again.

Delilah was nice. I once asked her why her parents had named her that. She told me that they'd once seen a movie called *Samson and Delilah*, one of those old Hollywood epics like *The Ten Commandments*, and her mother had fallen in love with the name.

I'd known Fran and Dan, the geometry twins, for two months before I realized they were great at track and field. We spent recesses racing down the soccer field. No matter how I tried, I just couldn't beat them. It must have been genetic. They kept asking if I'd had enough, but I wouldn't give in.

Kevin avoided me. Ever since we won the play competition it was as if, in his eyes, I didn't exist. And when his icy glance did by chance meet mine, his eyes would flick past me as if I wasn't there. It didn't bother me. Actually, I found it amusing. Sometimes I'd deliberately stand where he was sure to see me, and watch him pretend not to. But after about the hundredth time, I ignored him too.

He wasn't worth it. Things had really changed. He'd lost all his power to intimidate. Not only me, but anyone. I guess that happens. Premini said it was because I'd called his bluff. Something about being made fun of. And I wasn't a target anymore, because I wasn't alone anymore. She said guys like Kevin only pick on loners.

But even with Premini, Delilah, Fran and Dan, I missed Jenny. I longed to tell her about how well things were going.

She'd lied to me. She didn't write. She had my address, I didn't have hers. She hadn't been sure of it and she didn't want to ask her mother. Every day I checked the mail but found nothing.

Every day, on the way to school, I stood for a moment at the end of her street, listening to the wind moan. Ms. Roberts had moved to an apartment downtown. The house was for sale. The hole was still there in the screen door, the wire mesh twisting outward.

How was Jenny doing at her new school? How was she getting along with her grandfather? Was he mean? Had she changed her mind and tried to kill herself again? Had she succeeded this time? Why else wouldn't she write? I was too worried to be angry. I dreamed of her almost every night. Sometimes she was happy, smiling, telling me everything was fine. Sometimes I stood looking down over the edge of a high cliff, the clouds in turmoil, the wind freezing my breath, watching Jenny as she lay broken at the bottom, waves crashing around her, snatching at her wispy hair and tugging it down toward the ocean depths. I woke up screaming from those dreams.

At home things were a little better. Layla wasn't angry at me anymore. Not officially. But we didn't really talk. She said "Shab-khair" when she turned out the light. And sometimes she gave me instructions on how to do some chore or task, but nothing more than that. It would have bothered me before. I wouldn't have been able to stand it. I would have given in, and told her I was sorry. But now I just kept busy with other things.

Seema was close to Layla so I mostly avoided her. I played a lot with Waleed, though. He was fun. We played tag, and hide and seek. Kiddie games.

On the last day of school, I went up to Mr. Weiss and handed him a gift.

His cheeks stretched wide and he smiled. "Oh, Zainab, you didn't have to do that."

I grinned. "I wanted to. You've done so much for me the past year."

He shrugged, looking down at the rectangular package. "I've enjoyed watching you change. I think you'll do fine in high school. Which one are you going to?"

I smiled. "Glen Riverside High."

Mr. Weiss's bushy eyebrows shot up, like caterpillars doing pushups. I'd miss those eyebrows. He said, "Isn't that the same one Kevin's going to?"

I nodded. "Yeah. My older sister goes there too."

He puffed out his cheeks, and tilted his head, thoughtfully. "Did you ever think of going to Glen Hollow District?"

I couldn't believe it. "That old mausoleum? Why would I want to go there?"

Mr. Weiss frowned. "It's a fine school. It's the oldest one in the area."

I nodded. "And the hardest. I've heard that kids who get A's at Deanford get C's at Glen Hollow District."

"That may be true, but it will better prepare you for university. I think you can handle it. You'll learn so much more there than at Glen Riverside."

If Mr. Weiss thought it was good for me, maybe I should consider it. He'd been right about the play. I was so glad I'd done it. And though it wasn't exactly moving away from my past, going to Glen Hollow District would be a fresh start. Layla wouldn't be there to bug me. Nobody would know me, I could be whatever I wanted to be. Break free of the mold that Kevin and the others had held me in. The more I thought about it, the more I liked the idea.

Mr. Weiss was watching me. "Well?"

I smiled. "I like the idea. But is it too late?"

He grinned. "I can arrange it."

"Great." I gestured at the gift. "Open it."

He tore through the wrapping paper and lifted the lid of the box. With a twinkle in his eye, he withdrew the suspenders. "Thanks. I'll think of you whenever I wear them." He buckled them onto his pants.

I laughed. They looked nice, but I couldn't imagine Mr. Weiss not having to pull up his drooping pants.

It grew silent. Other kids were waiting outside to say goodbye to Mr. Weiss.

He smiled. "Take care of yourself, Zainab."

I nodded. "You too, Mr. Weiss."

He nodded back. "I will."

I had to leave then, the other kids were getting restless.

But one thing kind of cheered me up. I found out that Mr. Weiss had talked Premini and the geometry twins into going to Glen Hollow District too, so I wouldn't be totally on my own.

I left school that last day without intending to look back. Why should I? I would never enter that ugly, old, muddy yellow school again. But just as I was about to round the corner out of its sight, I gave in and turned for one final look.

It sat in a yellowish rectangular heap on the schoolyard. An ugly building. And yet whenever I passed it, on the way to my new high school, I knew I would think of Jenny.

I turned and started walking again, briskly. Why didn't she write? Had she forgotten all about me?

All that summer I waited for her letter. Filling the time with dozens and dozens of novels that I read in cramped closets, while Layla hunted all over the house for me to give me some chore to do.

When September came again, a new year at a new school, I felt like that man in the hadith. I had my own fresh start.

The first week of classes, I made friends with a vengeance. I still kept my old ones, but I made tons of new ones as well. I didn't want any of us Deanford kids to be singled out and targetted like I had been at my old school. I talked to everyone I met, and I encouraged Premini and the others to as well. Not everyone responded — I didn't expect them to — but the ones that did were the ones I worked on getting to know. Soon, I had built up such a good buffer zone that all the bullies left me alone.

A month after I started high school, after I'd had a chance to settle in to the routine, and long after I'd given up hope, I got a letter from Jenny —

Dear Zainab,

I'm so sorry I didn't write sooner but with the new school and the new place and all the adjustments, I just couldn't. I hope you'll forgive me.

Things are great on my grandfather's farm. I have a horse named Patches and a pig named Kevin. He's pink with silvery hair and he acts just like the real Kevin. He's always snuggling into my chest.

I've made some friends at school. I'm way out in the country so I have to take a bus and there's a girl my age, she's our neighbor, and she boards the bus at the same place I do. We're friends.

I've changed a lot. I guess I'm finally getting over Kevin. Though none of the boys around here interest me at all. I've been hitting the books and my marks are great. It's given me a completely different reputation around this school. I'm considered brainy.

My grandfather and I get along great. I'd lost touch with him because he and my mom never got along. I guess that's another thing we have in common. He's so gentle and shy. I think he was lonely before I came.

But I miss you. Maybe you could come out for a visit sometime. If you can't you've got to at least write.

I've got to go now. Lots of chores to do on a farm. Not much time for writing letters.

Bye for now,
Your friend always,
Jenny

In the top left corner of the envelope, there was a

return address. During class I snuck a moment here and there to write her back. I bought a stamp and envelope and mailed the letter on the way home.

And when I got to my house, I immediately went to the washroom to make wudu, for it was time to pray. I caught a glimpse of my face in the mirror. I looked different somehow. I'd changed. I seemed prettier. I knew I smiled easily, and often. I was smiling now. Then I stopped myself.

On impulse, I put on a sultry look and said to my reflection, "Dahling, if you luv me, would you please, please smile?"

I did smile. I even giggled. But, what the heck, I felt like it.